THE WRITER

Lori Osterberg

A Creative Standalone

Copyright © 2016 by Lori Osterberg.

All rights reserved. No part of this publication may be reproduced, distributed or transmitted in any form or by any means, including photocopying, recording, or other electronic or mechanical methods, without the prior written permission of the publisher, except in the case of brief quotations embodied in critical reviews and certain other noncommercial uses permitted by copyright law. For permission requests, write to the publisher, addressed "Attention: Permissions Coordinator," at the address below.

Vision Business Concepts Inc
4950 S Yosemite St F2-306
Greenwood Village CO 80111 USA
www.LoriOsterberg.com

Publisher's Note: This is a work of fiction. Names, characters, places, and incidents are a product of the author's imagination. Locales and public names are sometimes used for atmospheric purposes. Any resemblance to actual people, living or dead, or to businesses, companies, events, institutions, or locales is completely coincidental.

The Writer/ Lori Osterberg. -- 1st ed.
ISBN 978- 1539751601

Dedicated to creative women everywhere

Other Books by Lori Osterberg

~ The Creative Standalone Series ~

The Writer - Kelly & Aiden

~ The Choice Series ~

Destination Barcelona - Casey & Jordi
Destination Mexico City - Jena & Justin

Chapter One

She needed this workout. Bad.

He had her so mixed up. And so full of energy. She had no idea what to do with all of this pent up frustration.

Yeah, she was going with that. Frustration. She snorted knowing full well it wasn't just frustration.

She slid on her favorite workout shorts. Pulled the tank over her head and moved it into place. With a quick tie of her shoes, she was ready to go.

It was late; she was the only one in the gym. Tonight, intensity was her middle name.

One mile on the treadmill.
One hundred pull-ups.
One hundred pushups.
One hundred bodyweight squats.
Back to the treadmill for another mile.

She moved to the weights. And as she adjusted the barbell, she caught her breath. She knew he was there. Could feel him there.

She looked up, into the mirror, searching. Caught just a glimpse, in the corner, watching.

So he wanted to play that game?

She picked up the barbell, started in with the repetitions. Up. Down. Flexing. Moving.

She knew she looked good, standing there just a little sweaty, breathing hard.

Up. Down. Up. Down.

As she counted down ... seven, six, five, four ... she saw him move in.

He stepped to her side, searching for her eyes in the mirror.

He took her breath away. But she wasn't going to let him see how he impacted her. How bad she wanted him.

Three. Two. One.

She put the barbell back into place. And as she stood up, he was there. Behind her.

He wrapped an arm around her, pulled her in. He breathed deeply. "You're so fucking hot." He nibbled her neck, behind her ear, right where she liked it. Trailed his tongue down her spine.

She arched into him, moaned. How did he do that? How did he turn her into a quivering mess? How had she survived without him?

She pressed against him, feeling every last hard inch of him. Her hand traced down his abs, down his rock hard stomach. More. She wanted, oh, so much more ...

THE WRITER

"Dammit." Kelly jumped as her phone rang next to her. She picked it up, turned the volume down. She glanced at the incoming call, hit accept.

"Hi, Beth. What's up?"

"Hey, you, whatcha doing?"

"Writing."

"You're kidding, right? It's eighty degrees. It's Friday. It's time to play."

Kelly Sorenson reached up with her free hand, pinched the bridge of her nose, trying to determine how to keep the conversation from turning the way she knew it was about to go. She loved her friend, but lately, Beth had been on a personal mission to get her a life. And it was driving her crazy.

"Beth..."

"Nope, don't *Beth* me. It's Friday. It's beautiful outside. It's festival time. Come on; we're going out to have some fun. Todd's gone this weekend, and I don't want to eat alone. So you're coming with me. Meet me at Henry's at six!"

Kelly glanced at her watch. Four. That gave her two hours. She could easily make it. She glanced back at her computer, looking at where she'd left off. She'd written at least five thousand words in the last couple of hours, more than enough to keep her on schedule. She could probably squeeze in a few hundred more before she left.

"I hear your brain churning, wondering if you should tell me no and stay at home and work. The answer is no. Shut your computer down. Get dressed in something cute and meet me at Henry's. Or I'll come get you."

Kelly dropped her head to her hand. Closed her eyes and counted to five. She loved her friend. Beth Watson had been there through the thick of things these past few years. They'd met three years earlier at a writing convention, became inseparable in their few days together. Even after they both returned home, they started a routine of talking once a day, met when they could. They were like soul sisters. They thought alike. They could finish each other's sentences. Hell, they even wrote alike, collaborating on three books to date. But Beth's current mission was truly driving her crazy.

"If I meet you, it'll just be you, right? You don't have an ulterior motive, do you?"

"Geez, I set you up with one bad date, and you're all over me. That was last week. Forget it already. I told you I was sorry."

"Beth, he felt me up. In the restaurant. With you and Todd on the other side of the table. I'd known him for all of twenty minutes. He was a first class creep with a capital C. Never again, you got it?"

"Hey, I didn't expect him to do *that*. He's really nice at the club. Todd's played squash with him for months. I have no idea what his problem was."

"Honestly, I'm okay. I don't need a man in my life. I'm really *okay*."

"Kelly, I know you are. But I just think you work way too much. Trust me; no other writer can dare keep up with your schedule. You're a writing maniac. But you have to live too. You're too young just to sit in your house and write. You need to get out and have fun. You're only fifty-three years old. I know life's been rough since Tom. I get that. Having someone in your life again would be good for you. You're too young not to have the time of your life. Tom would want that for you, you know."

Kelly swallowed, pushing the knot that always formed in her throat back down. Tom. She missed him so much.

THE WRITER

Three years earlier, she and Tom had moved to Portland from San Francisco, partly to be nearer to their only daughter who had decided to make Portland home and partly for the opportunity Tom found to head a tech startup. They looked at it as their reinvention, their chance to do something fun and completely out of character.

And so Kelly wrote. She no longer needed a job - the startup bonus and stock option Tom had received ensured that. Her bucket list had always included a line item of becoming a famous novelist. So the move gave her the chance to write.

She nailed it. Killed it. Her first novel was an instant success. She'd hit Amazon and New York Times' best sellers lists within weeks.

They lived a fairytale life. They'd traveled every weekend, visiting Seattle, Vancouver, the coast. They explored the best restaurants. They found a quaint condo in the middle of the city center, remodeled it and called it home.

Then eighteen months later, Tom was on his way to a meeting. A young woman texted her friends, crossed the yellow line, and the fairytale ended, poof, in an instant.

Kelly couldn't have survived it without Beth.

Now she wasn't sure if she'd survive Beth. This dating thing truly was going to kill her. If she didn't kill Beth first.

"No, you can't kill me. It's against the law." Beth snickered, knowing full well what her friend had been thinking. "Come on. Let's meet at Henry's. You love it there. It's always lively, and they have great food. We can check out the latest happenings, watch the younger crowd hit on each other. It'll give us something to write about." If Beth knew anything, it was how to punch her friend's buttons.

"Well, when you put it like that ..." Kelly laughed. She loved Beth. And no matter what, she could never stay mad at her for more than a moment. Besides, the weather was truly beautiful. And since Henry's was only ten blocks from her condo, the walk would do her good. "Okay, six, I'll see you there in just a bit."

"Yeah. I'll see you there. Don't be late."

Chapter Two

"Hi, sorry I'm late." Kelly hugged her friend as she squeezed in beside her. She glanced around her. "This place is packed. How long until we're seated?"

"Crazy, right? Actually, you're right on time. I got here a little early anticipating it would be busy. We had a thirty-minute wait, and that was about twenty minutes ago." Beth glanced at her watch. "We should be seated soon. They're calling pretty quickly."

Kelly pulled her purse in as another couple tried to squeeze by. "I didn't know it got this wild. We should have picked someplace outside of town, further from the river."

Beth grinned. "Welcome to Fleet Week, baby. It's always crazy this time of year. Especially this year, the weather is unbelievable. It hit eighty today. This summer's going to be brutal." They watched as several men in uniform whooped and hollered to their left, at the bar. Beth snickered. "Gotta love Fleet Week. Livin' it up a little."

Kelly just rolled her eyes.

"I saw that." Beth looked at her sideways, fully aware of her expression. "You do remember livin' it up a little, right?" Beth looked at her pointedly, hoping to shake something loose in her friend.

"Geez, Beth, here you go again. You act like I never have any fun. I know how to have fun." And even as she said it, Kelly glanced down, trying desperately to avoid her friend's eyes.

"So I've been thinking …" Beth bumped Kelly's shoulders, clearly looking for a reaction she knew would come.

And here we go again.

"No." Kelly knew she had to put a stop to whatever Beth was thinking before she did something else crazy and embarrassing. "I left you too long here by yourself, didn't I?"

"I haven't even said anything." Beth gave an exasperated shrug.

"I know you. No."

"I know I've been pushing you a lot. But I care about you."

Kelly stared at her friend, knowing how lucky she was to have her. "I know you do." She reached out and gave her a quick hug.

With a smile from her friend, Beth used that as a launching pad to her new idea. "So I think it's time to jump in with both feet. Live a little. There's this group on Meetup a woman in my building was telling me about …"

Kelly tried the in-one-ear-out-the-other approach. *Meetup. Dating. Get a life. Wait, what?* "Wait, so you're saying I'm not living? Why do you keep insinuating that?" Kelly eyed her friend with a suspicious look.

Beth raised an eyebrow at her, questioning. "What'd you do last night?"

Kelly's skeptical glance gave way to a sheepish look, not wanting to answer.

"Well?"

"Write."

"And this morning?"

"Write."

"This afternoon?"

"Write."

"I rest my case."

"Come on, I like to write. That's not working."

"Kelly, I appreciate the fact you like to write. You're good at it. In fact, most people can't believe you've written six books over the past eighteen months with everything you've been through. Not only that, they're all bestsellers. They're good. Hell, they're great. I wish I could write like that, as fast as that. But you can't just live in book-world. You have to come out and play too."

"I do." Kelly tried to get the fire churning in her. *Fight. What she says can't be all true.* But she knew deep down inside that it was. Every last bit of it.

"You're fifty-three. You deserve a life. You know that, don't you?" Beth laid a hand across her best friend's. A warm squeeze told her she was on her side.

Kelly returned it with a weak smile. Still ...

"How do we get into this conversation all the time? I agreed to go out with that last friend of yours. You remember what a mess that was, right? And what about the guy before that? I thoroughly enjoyed hearing about his ailments all night long. You would have thought he was eighty-two instead of fifty-two." Kelly shuddered at the memories.

"But you always were so happy with Tom. You two did so well together. Don't you want that again?"

"I was happy with Tom because he was Tom. We had a life together, a history. I loved Tom because ..." She thought for a second. "Because he was Tom. I'm finally comfortable. Content. I have my daughter. I have my writing. I'm happy, as much as I can be. I had a man in my life, and I loved him. I loved him because he was Tom. Not just because he was a man. I don't need a man in my life. Not to be happy anyway. I just ..." Kelly stopped. She wasn't sure what to say next. Life had been so tough the past eighteen months. But it was getting better every day. She would always miss what she had with Tom. But it wasn't her norm anymore. She'd lived eighteen months without him. She was developing her own patterns, her own norm. And she was okay with it.

"When's the last time you crossed something off your bucket list?" Beth eyed her warily.

Kelly rolled her eyes. "I regret the day I told you about my bucket list."

"Not the point. When is the last time you crossed something off?"

Kelly tried to ignore Beth, but she couldn't help but think about it. She hadn't looked at it in a very long time. Not since Tom.

Beth snorted. "Yep, I knew it. You made that bucket list *with* Tom. It was about things the two of you wanted to do." She paused for effect. "You're just you now. You need one. You need to do things *just for you*. And I'm thinking you should do something really wild. I think you should add a one night stand to your bucket list. With a hottie. Like, let's pick up one of these cuties for you, right over here. Imagine living in storyland with one of *them*. I mean, look at them. Look at that hottie right there. If I weren't married ..."

THE WRITER

Kelly looked at Beth, turned and looked at the guy, back to Beth. "You're kidding right?"

Beth eyed her. "What? He's beautiful." She looked him up and down again. "Imagine how he could *influence* your writing? These guys are here for a week, then ship out to sea. It's the perfect chance to pick up a guy, knowing you won't have to see them ever again after this weekend. That's a way to get back in the saddle." Beth let her eyes drift around the crowded bar.

Kelly couldn't help but laugh. "Are you for real? You have looked around, haven't you? Now maybe if my twenty-four-year-old daughter were here, it would be something to consider. For *her*. I'm old enough to be their mothers. Every one of them. Look." She touched her friend's cheek, moving her line of vision to the bar where a dozen or more were standing.

"Not all of them." Beth returned the favor, placing a hand on her friend's cheek and pushing her attention to the two men checking in at the desk. "Fifty-somethings. High-ranking. And good looking."

Kelly stopped for just a moment. She had her there. Definitely good looking. Still. "And probably married."

"You never know. I don't see rings."

Over the noise coming from the bar, they heard their reservation called. "Watson, party of two."

Beth grabbed her friend's hand and made her way to the front. As she approached the desk, she made a quick decision. She asked the host, "Can we squeeze two more into the table you have for us?"

Kelly stuttered beside her. "Beth, no ..."

The host looked between the two, nodded her head. "Sure, it's a large table that can easily fit four."

Beth gave her friend a wicked smile. "Just a minute." And she disappeared to their right.

Kelly glanced at the host, turned and watched in horror as her friend approached the two men who had just checked in, nodded her head towards her, then led them both back to the front.

Beth winked at Kelly, said to the host, "Two more, please, lead away."

Kelly leaned in as they approached the table. "I'm going to kill you." All Beth did was snicker.

Chapter Three

The host showed them to their table, a large half circle booth near the back of the restaurant. Away from the crowds of the bar, it was quieter, a perfect place to relax.

Kelly slid in with Beth following. She found herself face to face, shoulder to shoulder, with a man even better looking than she'd noticed in the entryway. She glanced at his short dark blonde hair, the five o'clock shadow across his jaw. Enjoyed the way his eyes danced in the light. She scanned the insignia across his chest. *Nicely decorated. And very fit.*

She blushed as she put her attention on the menus as the host passed them around, telling them about the specials for the day.

"Well, I have to thank you both. We were looking at an hour wait. This is much better than standing in that tiny entry way. I'm Mike Jensen. My friend, Aiden Maddock." Mike nodded to his friend next to Kelly.

The introductions continued around the table.

"So what brings you two out on this lovely evening?" Beth joked with them, Fleet Week being the obvious reason.

Mike piped in. "A night off, beautiful weather, a great restaurant, what more is there? Thought we'd take in a bit of Portland before we ship out again on Monday. Are you two from Portland?"

"Born and raised," Beth said, then motioned to her friend. "She's only been a here a few years, one of the transplants that're making this city grow like crazy."

Aiden picked up the conversation. "So where were you from before landing here?"

Kelly looked up. "San Francisco. Moved here three years ago for a change of scenery."

"Do you like it? Do you think of Portland as home now?"

"Yes, actually I do. I've fallen in love with it. It has a lot of what the Bay Area did, but on a smaller scale. Friendlier people. Easier to get around. And such a raw beauty all around. I love being able to be out of the city in minutes."

That's why she'd been so quick to say yes to the move in the first place. That and being closer to her daughter. She loved being outside, finding new places to visit. Hiking had become her refuge as she recovered from Tom's death.

"So where's home for you? When you're not on a ship, that is?" Beth looked expectantly at both men.

Mike picked up the conversation. "San Diego. We've both been stationed there for years. Definitely home. I can't imagine moving any place else at this point."

Aiden nodded in agreement. "Can't image going back to snow every again." He winced at the thought.

Kelly laughed. "Hate snow, do you, Captain? Where are you from originally?"

THE WRITER

Aiden looked up in surprise. Few civilians knew Navy insignia enough to know rank. She obviously had some background. "Maryland originally. My dad was career Navy. Moved around a few times as a kid, but we settled in Maryland when I was in junior high, graduated there before moving to the Naval Academy."

Kelly nodded. She knew it well. "I grew up in Maryland as well. Canby, not far from Bethesda. We moved to the Bay Area right before tenth grade. My dad worked on satellites, had an opportunity for an executive position in Silicon Valley and jumped at it. I still have aunts, uncles, and cousins in Maryland, though I haven't been back in quite a few years."

"Small world. Guess we were neighbors for a while. My parents bought a house in Halton. That's where I lived, parents still do. " Though he hadn't been home in over a year. "That's how you know rank. I was wondering how you knew we were captains. Not everyone knows."

Kelly nodded. "Dad was pretty connected. They did a lot of parties, had a lot of guests over. And in Bethesda, as you know, that means military. I just picked it up, I guess. Never really thought much about it. Mom and Dad are still friends with quite a few high ranking officers, though they're all retired now. They head down to San Diego, have a small place on the beach where they meet some of their old buddies every year. Seems to be *the* place for military."

"Yep, filled with us." He laughed, knowing how true it was. All of his neighbors were either currently serving or retired.

"And I have to say I don't mind it, especially come the first of the year. It's a great escape when the rain sets in here. I met Mom and Dad this past January for a couple of weeks. The best." Kelly thought back to that trip. Another book kicked out in two weeks. It had been a productive trip.

The waiter stopped by. Mike ordered a bottle of chardonnay. They decided on an appetizer while they relaxed and took in the menus.

"So Canby, huh? There used to be a drive-in out on the edge of town." Aiden was trying to picture it, remember its location.

"Yes, that was where all the cool kids hung out. I moved after freshman year, so I never hung out at the Canby drive-in. Too young. I went to homecoming with Bobby Roberts freshman year, who promised he'd take me the next weekend. But he hooked up with Cami whatever-her-name-was, and I never went. Spent the weekend crying, imagining Bobby with Cami instead. Oh, the drama of high school." Kelly put her hand to her forehead in mock horror, then laughed at the old memories it brought back.

"High school. How'd we ever survive?"

Kelly picked up a sound in his voice that said he'd experienced his share of drama. "So you remember the drive in, spent a lot of time there, did you?"

Aiden blushed. "Maybe."

She smirked at the look in his eyes. "I get the picture. Clearly, you were one of *those* kids." She egged him on.

He shrugged his shoulders, something he couldn't deny. He'd taken more than his fair share of girls to the Canby drive-in on warm, summer nights.

"Then there was that old roadway diner not too far from there, where everybody would go after games. What was the name of that place?" Kelly turned to Aiden, felt a little unnerved watching the sparkle in his eyes.

"Mel's. Mel's Diner."

"You're right. Mel's. The greasy hamburgers, ugh. I still remember that taste. But the french fries, now those were french fries." Kelly touched her lips, thinking about all the baskets she'd shared with her friends.

"I know, right? I've never had anything like them since. I wonder what they put in them?"

"We probably don't want to know. It'd give us a heart attack today."

The waiter returned, set glasses in front of each, popped the cork on a bottle of chardonnay. Since Mike ordered, he passed the cork and a glass to him, waited for approval, then served.

"To a great dinner. Thanks for the invitation." The four clinked glasses, sipped and approved. They dove in hungrily to a plate of bruschetta, chatting about the events from the week before.

"Is this your first Fleet Week here in Portland?" Beth asked between bites.

Mike responded. "No, we were here, what five, six years ago?" He looked to his friend for confirmation.

Aiden nodded. "Something like that. It's the only other time I've been here. So whatever's walking distance from the ship, that's my perspective of what Portland has to offer."

"And what opinion have you formed, based on your ten, twelve block radius of Portland?" Kelly was curious what he thought. The mile or so leading up to the river where the ship was docked was interesting at best.

But if you knew where to look, were willing to look past some of the seediness that sometimes cropped up along the waterfront, there were so many interesting things to see and do. Kelly had explored it all, loved getting lost in the heart and the grit of the city. She loved the quaint little shops run by some of the most eclectic people she'd ever met. The Saturday Market? How could you not spend a fun-filled day there? Every block brought unexpected surprises, depending on the time of year you visited.

"Well ..." Aiden struggled for what to say. He glanced at Mike for help and was rewarded with a smirk. He wasn't getting any help from that direction. With three pairs of eyes on him, he started "Portland's ... interesting."

Both Beth and Kelly broke out into laughter.

Kelly was first to recover. "If you would have said anything different, I would have wondered. Never base your opinion of Portland merely on these few blocks. Especially this time of the year. There's so much more."

"So blue hair, VooDoo Donuts, and free-flowing pot isn't a part of everyone's lifestyle?"

"Nope. Never had blue hair, always been a blond." Kelly pointed to her hair. "Pot? Well, I plead the fifth on that one. I did go to college in San Francisco after all. And VooDoo Donuts? They're an acquired taste." Was she really flirting with him? He seemed to make it so easy.

Kelly glanced at Beth. It was written all over her face. She approved. Big time.

Aiden continued. "Well, the guys seemed to like them." His eyes returning to Mike, who nodded. "What were they eating this morning? One had bacon on it. One had fruit loops."

Mike added, "Oreos or something. And then that one looked like a gingerbread man ..."

Kelly smiled. "Yep, that's the VooDoo special. You get a pretzel stake to stab it with. Hence, where VooDoo comes from."

"Oh, now I get it. Anderson kept stabbing at that thing. I was wondering what he was doing."

"It's jelly filled. So the 'blood' runs out of it when you stab it."

THE WRITER

"Sick. That's kind of twisted." Aiden scratched his head, wondering what he was missing.

"I told you. An acquired taste. The kids love them. My daughter eats them all the time."

The waiter stopped by to check in, filled the water glasses, took their orders.

Mike picked up his phone, checked the screen, looked at Aiden. "It's Janet, gotta take this."

Aiden nodded, watched him head towards the back. "His wife." He looked apologetically to Beth.

Beth nodded. "That's cool. I'm married too; my husband's out of town for the weekend. I get it."

Kelly glanced at Aiden. "You married?"

She saw a hint of sadness settle in his eyes. "No. You?"

She returned the look. "No."

With movement at the end of the table, Kelly watched Beth warily as she saw her attitude change, saw a glimmer in her eye. Then watched as she rose.

"I'll be back." Beth disappeared towards the back, following in Mike's footsteps.

Kelly scratched her forehead, just a little worried about what her friend was concocting.

"So you said daughter. You have a daughter? Just the one?" Aiden took a sip of wine, sat back and relaxed. He looked expectantly at Kelly.

"Yes. Taylor. She's twenty-four, a good kid. She went to school at University of Oregon, found a job here in Portland. It's in the food industry; they make a vegan cheese. Good stuff, actually. She loves it here too. She moved in with her boyfriend a few months ago. They're happy, so I'm happy." She smiled. "You? You have kids?"

"Yep. Two myself. Ashley is twenty-three, Hannah's twenty-one. Ashley works at a winery up in Sonoma County. Hannah is still in school at Arizona State. She always liked it hot, said San Diego just wasn't warm enough for her. She seems happy in Phoenix; we'll see if she sticks it out after she graduates next year."

"Three successful kids. Can't ask for much more." She tipped her glass to his, and they drank.

"So a winery? That must be exciting. I love wine country. Always seemed like such a dream job, almost romantic. Does your daughter like it?"

"She does. I have no idea where she came up with it, but she studied wine business and viticulture at Cal Poly. Graduated and walked into her dream job, or so she says. She's been there about eight months now, still loves it. It is beautiful; I'll give her that much."

"What does she do?"

"She's in marketing, event production. She's in charge of setting up all the events they hold throughout the year. Well, she's on the team. I won't say in charge really. She works with about a half-dozen or so. Good group of people. She's learning a lot." Aiden sat up, leaned into her. "So I gotta ask. A vegan cheese? Tell me more."

She laughed. "It's very good stuff. It's a cheese spread, comes in a jar. You can find it in the dairy section of places like Whole Foods. It's made from cashews. So it's good for you and tastes good too. I've made mac n cheese with it; you can't really tell the difference. It's that good."

"Wow. Who knew? I'm really not in touch with that kind of stuff. I eat on the ship. Go out when I'm home."

"Not much of a cook, are you?"

"That would be no. You?"

THE WRITER

"I love to cook. Though I'll admit, I don't do much of it for one. But I love to play around and try new things. I work out of my home, so I have the time to play. My daughter and her boyfriend invariably show up several times a week, so I send them home with leftovers."

"So you work at home? What do you do?"

"I'm a writer."

Mike and Beth came back to the table together, almost breathless. And from the look on their faces, Kelly knew she was in trouble. She waited for whatever deal the two had concocted together. And sure enough, it began.

With Mike.

"So I hate to do this to you, but I gotta go. Something came up back on the ship. But you stay, have fun."

Beth continued, "Yeah, I gotta go too. Todd called, gotta get home, need to check on something."

The two mumbled on and on while Aiden and Kelly stared. Glared. *Really?*

And as the two rushed away from the table, out of the restaurant, Aiden and Kelly turned back and stared at each other.

Then burst out laughing.

"Did that just feel like the world's biggest and worst setup ever?"

"I know I'm bad at this, but yeah. I can't believe Mike did that. I guess your friend Beth must be made from the same mold."

If he only knew.

"I'm going to kill her tomorrow."

Seriously. Kelly started envisioning ways of getting back at her supposed best friend. Why was she always so serious about trying to set her up? And right here, right now, with a guy she'd just met?

Aiden cut into her thoughts. "Nah, let her sweat. Don't say anything; it'll drive her crazy."

That's one approach.

"Oh, I like the way you think. You've got a mean streak, don't you, Captain Maddock?"

He chuckled. "Mike likes to keep me on my toes. I work hard to pay him the favor." He stared into her eyes, clearly enjoying what he saw.

She held his gaze, and for just a moment, fought back the thought that she was secretly glad Mike and Beth had disappeared.

He continued. "Well, we're here. We might as well stay and eat. If you're up to it and don't mind eating with me tonight."

She tipped her head towards him, flirting with him just a little. "I'd love that." She caught herself, heard herself saying those words. Felt her own femininity coming into play. Wondered where on earth this feeling had come from. It'd been all work for so long. Could she actually have a good time with someone of the male persuasion?

Could she actually ... *date?*

She scowled, thinking of what Beth had been telling her for weeks.

The look didn't go unnoticed. "If you'd rather leave, I understand." Aiden didn't want to hold her here against her will.

Kelly jumped. "Oh no, I didn't mean that at all. I was just thinking. Beth has been telling me to get out and live a little for weeks now. I always ignored her. And I just realized she might be right."

She looked him squarely in the eyes. "And if you ever tell her I said that I will have to kill you for it."

He zipped his lip. "Your secret's safe with me."

Chapter Four

"I guess we might as well start with the obvious. With the big elephant in the room. You're obviously single, and your friend thinks you need to be set up. Because clearly Mike and Beth conspired back there with that dramatic exit they just pulled. Am I right?"

"Probably. Mike's been trying to get me out for months now."

"Funny, Beth too. Married friends aren't happy unless you're married too. Are you divorced?"

Kelly saw a hint of sadness pass over his eyes. She had enough of it in her own system to recognize grief for what it is. The lines in his forehead. The deep breath before he began.

"Widower. Eighteen months now. Mike thinks I need to move on. I guess in some ways I think I do too. I just haven't had the opportunity."

Kelly sucked in her breath, trying to absorb this tiny piece of news. She laid a hand on his arm. "I'm sorry."

She felt for him. She truly did. She saw herself in so many ways. The way he breathed in deeply, trying to avoid a flare of panic. Trying to overcome the overwhelming urge to get up and run. And above it all, the small internal nod as if doing so would keep it all together. All of it were feelings she knew all too well. At this table, she knew she wasn't alone in her pain of losing a spouse. She saw it written all over his face.

She took a deep breath, let out a sigh before she began.

"This is going to sound so strange, but I'm a widow too. It's just coming up on eighteen months for me as well. I know just how you feel."

He almost didn't believe her until he looked up into her eyes and knew it was true. Could feel it was true. He moved his hand, laid his over hers. "I'm sorry."

That sat there, searching, looking at each other, as if trying to register what the words really meant.

Could they both be in the same circumstance? What were the chances? What were the odds? Still, they could see it in each other's eyes.

She swallowed again and continued. "Eighteen months. You said eighteen months ..."

"Yes. Eighteen months. December second," he whispered with a catch in his voice.

Was this for real? Kelly felt a tingle pass over her, between them. Kindred spirits in the worst possible way. "November twenty-seventh."

"Fuck."

"Yeah, fuck." She brought her eyes back up to his.

"How?" Aiden was suddenly curious about this woman sitting beside of him. He could see the pain, wondered how he missed it before.

THE WRITER

"Car accident. He left one morning and didn't come home. Kissed me goodbye to head off to a meeting. A twenty-five-year-old woman texted her friend that she was running late. She crossed the line, each doing sixty miles an hour. Both of them died instantly. Not much left of their cars. Cars don't do so well when they slam into one another at that speed and roll again and again. And just like that, I lost my husband of twenty-five years in an instant."

The tears welled in her eyes. One lone tear fell down her cheek.

So much pain. No matter how much time went by, the pain was always there. She'd perfected her death elevator speech, as she liked to call it. Unfortunately, she gave it all too frequently. That alone should have made the process easier. But it never did.

Then he did something no one had ever done before.

He didn't say anything. He didn't have to.

Aiden laced his fingers with hers, gave them a squeeze and a feeling passed between them. A gentle acknowledgment that he understood some of what she had gone through.

She took a deep breath. Wiped away the tear and turned her attention to him. "You?" Now that her well-rehearsed speech was out of the way, she was curious about his story.

A deep breath. A swipe of the hand across his face. Composure, she knew he was setting the stage.

"Cancer. She was diagnosed with melanoma and three months later she was gone. We had our good and bad days, but mostly the worst. Because it all went from bad to worse so quickly. We had plans, you know? And cancer wasn't part of it. You just deal with it, no choice. And then it's over, and you have to move on." He pushed his fingers through his hair.

Stared at the ceiling for just a moment, trying to catch his breath.

She waited until he looked back at her. "So you know how you just look at people when they say the stupidest things. Like, 'At least he went quickly' or my personal favorite, "He's in a better place", and all you want to do is run away screaming? Because really, *is* he in a better place, rather than being here, enjoying our time together, enjoying his daughter, watching her finish college and move into her own life? Or any of the other mindless things people say when they're trying to sympathize, empathize with you, because they truly have no idea what you're going through? Well, in this case, I can honestly say I think we both have some idea. Not a good club to be in."

They stared. They blinked. They acknowledged. All while an unbelievably powerful bolt of electricity jolted between them. Or so Kelly thought. It made her tingle inside.

Aiden searched for the right words. "So what's that quote? Of all the gin joints in all the world ..."

"In all the towns in all the world ..." She corrected.

"She walks into mine." They finished together, laughing.

"Weird, huh?" He looked at her.

"Yeah. What are the chances?" She stared back into eyes.

"Who ordered the salmon?" the waiter asked.

"We'll take the check please," Aiden said to the waiter as she refilled their water glasses.

"The gentleman here with you earlier picked up the tab. He said to put everything on his card, so you're set to go."

"Really?" Aiden felt a sly smile spread across his face. "Hold on," he looked from the waiter to Kelly. "Since dinner is on my friend tonight, care for another bottle of wine and dessert?"

"Ooh, I like the way you think. Sounds great to me."

Aiden looked back at the waiter. "Another bottle of wine," he pointed to his glass. "And every dessert on the menu. Just put it on my friend's tab. Thanks."

He leaned back with a satisfied grin on his face. "Serves the bastard right. I was going to kill him tonight. I may still do it anyway. At least now I know he'll feel the pain when his wife raises hell over spending so much money in one restaurant."

"Still. Every dessert on the menu? What are we going to do with that much dessert?" She looked over at him, admiring the way his eyes lit up as he spoke.

"Eat what you want. I'll box up everything leftover and bring it back with me. Trust me, on a ship, I'll be lucky if I get it on board before someone inhales it."

The waiter returned with a bottle of chardonnay, uncorked it and poured into each of their glasses.

Aiden picked up his glass, held it out to hers.

"To getting back at our *supposed* best friends." They toasted and laughed as Kelly's phone buzzed on the table.

She glanced down and read.

Oh, the night kept getting better.

Are you okay?

She smirked at the words, finding it funny that her friend suddenly grew a conscience.

"So it seems my friend is suddenly worried about me." She held it out to Aiden for him to read.

"Seems like the co-conspirators are feeling guilty." Aiden held out his own phone for her to read.

Everything okay?

Kelly glanced at Aiden. "Okay, let's have some fun with this." She quickly typed.

Are you kidding? You left me with a monster. I think he's a serial killer or something.

"Hey." He pretended to be offended, but couldn't keep the chuckle inside. The response was almost instantaneous.

What?! What happened?

And almost at the same moment, Aiden's phone beeped.

Is everything all right?

They burst out laughing. Only stopped as seven large desserts were placed in front of them.

"Hey, could you do me a favor?" Aiden looked up at the waiter as he punched a few buttons on his phone. "Could you take a picture of us? Make sure you get the bottle of wine and the desserts in the photo too." Aiden reached an arm around Kelly's shoulders, bottle in hand. He held up a glass to her; she returned touching her rim to his. They leaned in, touching cheeks, hamming it up for the photo.

"Here you go." The waiter handed Aiden back his phone. He pulled it up, showed it to Kelly. "Hey, not bad."

With a few more touches, he sent it off to Mike with one word.

Thanks.

THE WRITER

"That should keep them quiet for a while." He turned off his phone and tucked it into his pocket. He turned his attention back to Kelly.

"All joking aside, I really have had a great time tonight." Aiden studied her face, clearly noticing the way she was looking at him.

"Me too." Kelly matched his eye movements, studying his eyes, his mouth.

She swayed a little as she took him in. She'd had a couple of glasses of wine. But clearly, there was more going on at the table than a little wine. She'd been out of the circuit for a long time. But she wasn't dead. She hadn't looked at a guy as she was clearly looking at Aiden since her husband. A part of her wondered what it would be like to take the next step. She'd have to think about that. Later. Alone. In her bed. *Alone.*

"Okay, here." She handed him a fork. "We've got to at least try a little of each of these. What's your favorite? Chocolate? Berries? I think this one has apples in it." She picked up a plate, lifting it up to analyze what was under the crust.

He watched her; she felt his eyes were on her, searching. She sensed it in his rhythm. The heat he was putting out next to her was enough to ignite the table. She wouldn't look back, couldn't look back, scared of what would happen. They'd crossed a line. They'd moved from casually meeting at the front of the restaurant, to finding each other more than just a little attractive.

Her mind spun trying to figure out how that part of her brain kicked into gear after eighteen months of hibernation.

She'd loved flirting with her husband. Loved the passion that had followed them into their empty-nest years. Some couples never survived their kids leaving. For Kelly and Tom, their love life had kicked into high gear, thoroughly enjoying the freedom that came with an exciting new lifestyle in an exciting new place. They'd courted each other with zealous behavior. In some ways, it had been like dating all over again.

It died with her husband.

But suddenly, she felt a burning way deep inside. Something that said it might be time to let it bubble up once again.

She moved a little closer as she reached for a bowl.

"Look at the size of these berries." She held it up for him to see. Met his eyes and held for just a moment.

Something in his eyes said he wanted something way more delicious than anything the dessert menu had to offer.

But for now, he'd settle for dessert. With her.

He grabbed a fork, touching her fingers as he slid the bowl from her grasp. "Berries. Definitely berries."

She moved the berry shortcake front and center. They each took a bite.

"Oh, God that's good."

"Did you get the ice cream? Add some ice cream."

Aiden took another bite, this time with ice cream.

"Even better."

"Okay, enough of that one. Try the chocolate cake." Kelly moved the plate closer, cutting a small piece off the corner.

"Mmm ..." She licked her lips, rolling her eyes as she tasted the dark chocolate. Mixed with the berry flavor from earlier, it was simply divine.

"Here, try this. But make sure you get the berries with it." She pushed the two plates closer so he could mix the two.

"Agreed. That's good. Maybe we should tell them in the back and have them create something new. Berry chocolate cake. It could be a winner." He scooped up another berry and added it to another bit of chocolate cake. He savored it. "Yep, that's good."

THE WRITER

They made their way through another dozen bites of dessert, then sat back and enjoyed the last of the bottle of wine.

As the tables around them began clearing out, they agreed it was finally time to leave.

"Is your car around here? Let me walk you to your car." Aiden wasn't sure how she had gotten here, but wanted to make sure she got home safe. While neither of them were drunk, they had shared several glasses of wine over four hours of dinner.

"No, I walked. I'm only ten blocks up from here."

"I'll walk you home." Since it was after ten, he suddenly felt protective of keeping her safe.

"No, really. It's in the opposite direction of where you're going. I can't ask you to do that."

"You didn't ask. And I'm doing it. It's the least I could do after the evening we've shared." He placed his hand on the small of her back as he opened up the door for her to head outside.

She couldn't help but feel the tingle he gave her every time he came into contact with her. She could have blamed it on the wine. But she wasn't naive enough to think that made any difference. She was positive it was all him.

"Okay, I accept. But I'll call Uber for you. That way you don't have to walk miles back to the ship."

"Really, not necessary."

"Yes, it is. It's the only way you're coming with me." She eyed him, telling him she was serious.

"Okay, deal."

She tucked her arm under his, and they walked the distance while she gave him a tour of the surrounding buildings along the way. With its quirky shops, elaborate architecture, and people watching in abundance, they chattered endlessly about what made Portland unique. This was her city, a place she explored endlessly on foot. And she knew every inch of the streets between the restaurant and her condo well.

She stopped in front of a high-rise that towered above. She turned, facing him once again.

"Well, this is me." She shrugged a shoulder towards the front door.

"Thanks for the walk. Let me call." Kelly pulled up Uber on her phone, punched in a few buttons, and flipped it back into her purse. "They should be here in a few minutes."

She took a deep breath, suddenly desperate for a few extra minutes to be with him. Her brain searched for ways to extend their time together. Knowing full well he was heading out to sea in just a couple of days. *Impossible.*

Grasping, she said the only thing that came to mind. "So, tomorrow. You have any free time tomorrow?"

She saw relief flood his eyes.

Aiden clearly hadn't wanted the night to end either. "Yeah, I'm off at four. Have the evening open if you're up to another dinner with me. I could pick you up. Or meet you somewhere. I'm open for ideas - I don't have much knowledge of the area."

A chance. A chance to be with him. A chance to learn more about him. A chance to explore whatever this was between them. Kelly pulled her thoughts together, gathering up her courage to take one of the biggest steps she'd taken in a very long time.

"When's the last time you had a home cooked meal?"

Aiden stopped to think. He searched, trying to remember the last time he'd been at home for dinner. Or anyone's home for that matter.

Kelly laughed. "That long, huh?"

Aiden chuckled. "I guess it's been awhile."

THE WRITER

"How would you like to come for dinner? I can whip up a pretty mean home cooked meal. I can give you views of Portland from the tenth floor. I could even be persuaded to throw in some berries for dessert." She batted her eyelashes at him. "I mean, I think I can trust you're not a serial killer, right?" She teased, clearly flirting with him, hoping he'd say yes.

She was rewarded with a nod of his head and a hand reaching out for hers.

"How could I ever turn that down? Done. I'll be here. What time?"

"Whenever. If you're off at four, come any time after. Put my number and address in your phone." She gave him the numbers while he punched it in. He tucked his phone back into his pocket once again.

Their eyes danced as they took each other in, learning, searching, seeing things in each other that hadn't surfaced in a long time.

"Kelly, I'm really looking forward to it." Aiden moved closer, touched her fingers. "For a night that started out in a very awkward way, I'm grateful for how well it's turned out. Thanks for having dinner with me."

He leaned, searching her eyes as he drew closer. Then ever so slowly, he brushed his lips over hers, tasting. He lingered, closed his eyes for just a moment. He braced himself with a hand on her arm, heady from the experience that very quickly rocked his world.

She pulled away, ever so slightly. Returned her gaze to his as she drank him in.

"Thank you for one of the best nights I've had in a long time. For dessert. For the walk. For everything." She placed a hand gently on his chest. "I can't wait for tomorrow evening."

She leaned in one more time, captured his lips with her own.

They lingered, nibbling, enjoying the taste.

A car pulled up near the front of the building. A signal it was time to go.

She pulled away. "I guess I should go. Up. I mean upstairs. To my home." Kelly was tongue-tied, flustered by her feelings for him.

Part of her wanted more, full force. The other part needed a break. She wanted desperately to analyze these feelings that had crept up on her out of nowhere. For someone who had been head over heels in love for years, decades, she suddenly felt like a novice once again.

She'd written books on this, for crying out loud. She'd studied love every which way to Sunday by watching movies and taking in people around her. But this was new. And dammit if it didn't feel absolutely incredible.

"Tomorrow." Aiden agreed, clearly tongue-tied himself. He backed up, watching her. Made his way to the car that was now outside of her doors.

"I'll see you then." She struggled to fit the key in her door.

"Good night, Kelly." He closed the door and waved one last time.

She watched as he rode away.

"Damn." She said it to no one in particular. Kelly reached up, touching her fingers to her lips, relishing the feeling he'd left behind.

Tomorrow couldn't come quick enough.

Chapter Five

Aiden rose at four, threw on his shorts and made his way down to the gym. Thirty minutes on the treadmill, followed by thirty minutes of lifting weights left him invigorated for the day ahead.

Like he needed that. He knew only one thing had him going for the day ahead. Kelly.

He grabbed his water bottle, sucked down what was left, turned to fill it up again as he noticed Mike walking in.

Aiden sneaked behind him, putting him in a chokehold. "Hey asshole, what were you thinking last night?" He pretended to be mad.

Mike wiggled free. "Sorry, just thought you could use some time with someone other than what this cruise has to offer." He studied his friend, weighing how pissed he truly was.

"Yeah, well don't do it again. It could have been a disaster."

"Sorry, man. I was just having fun. It was her friend's idea as much as mine. She caught me back by the bathroom, thought it would be good to try and get her friend out into the dating world as well. I won't do it again." Mike almost felt a little sorry that he'd put his friend in a bad situation. "So, it didn't work out?"

"I didn't say that. You just have to suffer." Aiden smiled as he turned for the door.

It took a second for it to register. Then Mike was in hot pursuit. "What do you mean? It did work out? Did you have a good night?" He moved in front of his friend, blocked him, judged the look in his eyes. "Did you get some last night?"

"Stop already. It's not like that." But no matter what he did, Aiden couldn't hold back the grin. "But I do have another date tonight. She invited me back to her house. A home cooked meal. She lives downtown, tenth floor. Promised me a spectacular view of the skyline." Aiden shouldered by his friend, trying to break free of the conversation.

"Wait. Wait a minute. You have a date?" Mike rushed to keep up. "Really?"

"Gee, don't sound so surprised. I'm not that bad, am I?" Aiden would do anything to make Mike sweat at this point.

"No, of course not. I didn't mean that. It's just, really? You have a date? You're seeing her again?"

"Yes. Today. After work."

"Really?"

"Enough. Yes, really. Now can I go and get ready or what?" He looked hard at his friend. But he was in too good of a mood to look anything but happy.

"All right, buddy. Have fun. I'm excited for you. I mean that."

Mike knew how difficult Aiden's life had been in the past two years. He'd been there for him in the thick of it all. He'd been there when Aiden broke down after Michelle's diagnosis.

He'd been there when she was admitted to hospice. He'd been there when she'd died. He'd been there when Aiden collapsed in his arms, wishing death upon himself. He'd nursed him along, often doing both jobs on deck as efficiently as one. He'd carried him through it all.

He was like a brother to him. He'd do anything for him. He wanted to see him whole once again.

Mike smiled, watching him walk away. Maybe he was on his way, finally. That alone was worth the restaurant tab from the night before. Even if his wife had been pissed.

Aiden watched as the clock ticked slowly by. He'd never known time could move so slowly.

The day before they headed out to sea always brought on a host of problems. Today was no different. He dealt with minor emergencies all day long.

A little after four, he made his way back to his room, showered and shaved.

He tapped Uber for a ride.

He stopped and picked up a bottle of chardonnay. A little after five, he arrived.

Aiden pushed the buzzer. Heard her familiar voice on the other end.

"Hello? Aiden?"

"Hi, yep it's me."

"Come on up. I'm in the kitchen. Door's open."

Aiden took the elevator, found her door and entered.

She wasn't kidding. The panorama of the skyline was incredible. He walked over, took in the view. Noticed the music softly playing in the background. *Nice.*

"Hi." Aiden came in behind her, set the bottle of wine on the counter. "You weren't kidding. This is spectacular."

"Hi," Kelly smiled at him, followed his line of vision out her windows. "I told you, I don't disappoint. This place was a wreck when we bought it. A woman had owned it for years without putting an ounce of maintenance work into it. The kitchen was an awful-retro-seventies mess; the carpets were disgusting. But the view ... We couldn't get over the view and knew we could fix the rest. It was my *hobby* for six months."

She returned her gaze to him. "How are you today?" He looked tired.

"Good. Great, actually, now that I'm here." He couldn't help but stare at her. He also couldn't stop himself from leaning in and brushing his lips against hers. And lingering for just a bit.

"Thanks for the wine. Is it chilled? I have a couple in the refrigerator as well. Want to choose one and pour? Corkscrew is over there by the fridge." She motioned towards the drawer.

Aiden rummaged through until he found what he was looking for. Selected a bottle and poured. Moved a little closer to her. "What can I do to help?" He didn't get in the kitchen much anymore. But there was something familiar about working together, cooking a meal with someone he enjoyed spending time with.

"You said you like everything. I'm making Pad Thai. I hope that's okay."

"Perfect."

"Like it with tofu?" She smiled at the look on his face.

"Tofu?"

"Oh, come on, Captain Maddock. You've never had tofu before?" She laughed at his wrinkled nose.

"Now why would I do that when there are so many other things to eat out there?" He looked at it again. "Tofu, huh?"

THE WRITER

Kelly bumped her hip against his. "Yes, tofu. You're in Portland now. Tofu. It's good for you. Healthy. I promise you'll love it. I have a special way of cooking it."

At the moment, he didn't care what he ate. Aiden sipped his wine, watching her cut, slice and mix everything together. She added the tofu to a hot pan, stirred it until crispy. She transferred it to a plate to cool.

Then forked a piece, dipped it in sauce, moved in close. "Here, try." She moved it up to his lips.

He tasted it. "Wow. Okay, that's not half bad."

"See? Told you so."

She placed the noodles on plates, sprinkled it with peanuts, added the tofu. "Want to grab the wine and follow me out?"

Kelly set down the plates. They grabbed chairs, settled in for an evening of good food, great wine, and even better conversation.

"So how long have you lived here?"

"Just over two years. We moved up here from San Francisco when Tom got a new job. Our daughter was here in college; we wanted a change. He jumped at a start-up opportunity here. I can write from anywhere, so it seemed like a logical choice. We rented when we first got here while we tried to settle on where we wanted to live. We always kept coming downtown and eventually found this place. It's an older building, but I love its location. It's also bigger than the places they're building now. We remodeled the kitchen and bathrooms, new flooring, so it's perfect. I wouldn't trade it. I'm really happy here."

"It seems central. Great walking city. At least that's the way it seemed last night."

"Exactly. This street right here," Kelly motioned to the street off to her left. "This is one of the main drags. Everything you need is blocks away. Shopping. Restaurants. Trader Joe's. I mean, who can live without Trader Joe's, right?"

He laughed. "Not me." Though he knew he hadn't set foot in one since Michelle died. He hadn't done much of anything since that day. He was either on a ship, at a friend's, or in a restaurant. *Maybe it was time to change.*

"So you mentioned last night you're a writer. What do you write?" He watched as she gave him an inquisitive look.

Kelly bit her lip. "I'm an author. Novels. I have over a dozen published." She waited for his response.

He sat back, impressed. He grabbed his wine, truly wanting to find out more about what she wrote. "Novels? Anything I'd know?"

She laughed. "Um, probably not. I write romance." She chuckled as she saw the look that crossed his eyes. "I take it you don't read much romance?"

"Caught me there. I think my wife did. She always had books lying around."

"Danielle Steele, Nora Roberts. You might know their books. They have hundreds between them."

"If you say so. I hate to say it, but I don't read a whole lot. Definitely not romance. If I do have a chance to pick up something, it's usually a mystery. Maybe a military novel." He grinned.

"Ah, stereotypical. The captain reads war novels." She shook her head eyeing him slyly as she said it.

"Tom Clancey, James Patterson. I read a Harlan Coben not long ago and really liked it."

"I like him too. I love how he twists current topics into his plots."

Aiden sat back reflecting on her skills. There were so many questions that crossed his mind. He had no idea where to start.

THE WRITER

So he started with the obvious. "So back to the romance, you do this for a living?"

She chuckled. "Yes, it pays well. Do you have any idea how rabid women are over their romance novels? And the good thing about it, they buy and buy and buy. Once a book is done, you need another. And if you're a writer like me who writes book after book after book, if you create a following, you have instant sales the moment you release a new book. It's really a very good business model. And it's made me a lot of money over the last three years."

"Hmm. Very interesting. Very impressive, too. Maybe I'll have to read one and check out your writing style."

She envisioned him there on his ship, at sea, holding up one of her paperbacks as he lounged in the cafeteria. Kelly got up from the table, went to her office and grabbed several of her recent titles. She laid them out in front of him. In typical romance style, they had lovers lounging on beaches, in hammocks and cuddling in each other's arms.

"Think you could read one of these on your ship?" She laughed at his look. "I'd give you one, but you might be better off reading it on your Kindle if you have one."

She leaned in, rested a hand on his arm. "Seriously, I know the stigma that goes along with the romance industry. But I love it. I get to play with my characters every day. I have a lot of fans who adore what I do. And I can honestly say I have the best job in the world. And the pay is great. In my life, this works very well for me. I'm happy, at least with this side of things. In many ways, it's helped get back to where I am today.

"It took me a few months before I could even write again. But my fans were all there for me. Then about a year ago, I poured out a book on death and finding romance all over again. I did it in less than three weeks. Pent up anger, frustration, and guilt all at once, I guess." She frowned at the memory. Shook it off with a flick of her hand and returned her gaze to his.

"Anyway, I produced it, and it was almost perfect. Very little editing. We got it to market and women fell for it. It's translated into eighteen languages. It shot to the top of the charts, and it's still a best seller today. " She shuffled the books, laid *Finding Love Again* on top.

"This was my coming-back-to-life therapy. This book changed things for me. Now I'm not saying I don't have plenty of bad days, but I'm getting there."

Aiden picked up the book, read the back cover. Even the words on the back touched him to the very core. They echoed true with many of the things he'd felt over the past eighteen months. And knowing what he knew about Kelly already, he knew she spoke from the heart.

"I don't even know what to say."

Kelly stood before him. "Then don't. I think we've had enough work talk. It's still beautiful out. Still early. Ever seen the Rose Garden here?"

Aiden laid the book down, stood up next to her. "Nope. I've only been to Portland the one other time. Didn't get out of downtown. Didn't have a reason to."

"Well, I'm giving you a reason. It's a short walk from here. How about if we go and tour the gardens, then come back here for that blackberry dessert I promised you?" She looked at him expectantly.

"Sounds perfect."

CHAPTER SIX

Kelly fell in line with his steps, inched next to him and laced her fingers with his as they walked. Even though Portland had only been her home for a few years, she spoke of the things she'd fallen in love with almost from the beginning.

They climbed the stairs into the park, made their way around the trees and onto the path that led to the gardens.

"So the one thing I love about coming from this angle is how the roses overwhelm you. You don't see them; they aren't there." They walked a few more steps, and she stopped. "And now they are."

"Wow."

"I know, right?"

"That's incredible."

"You don't know where to look, do you? The color. The roses are everywhere. And look," she pointed between the trees. "It's Mt Hood over there. You can't always see it, but it's so clear tonight. Beautiful."

She watched as he took it all in. She thought back to her first visit and how much she'd fallen in love with this very spot. She'd stood here, visited hour after hour that first year. It still made her heart skip a beat at the view.

"Come on." Kelly pulled him to the stairs.

Thousands upon thousands of roses lay before them. They wound their way through every section, taking in each bloom before they moved on to the next. Plots of roses in every color of the rainbow. Yellows, pinks, oranges, purples, reds, whites. The color combinations seemed endless. They visited the teacup and miniature collections. Walked under trellises with roses hanging from up above.

"Ohmigod, you have to smell this one. Delightful, isn't it?"

"Look at these buds. Perfection."

They both had their phones out, snapping photos of each rose that offered a different color, a different style, a different pattern.

"This one. This one right here is the best."

"No. You're wrong. It's this one."

They fell into a game of trying to choose the perfect rose. And of course, every plot brought something to compete with, a rose that had just a little more to offer.

They laughed as they compared notes, trying to pressure each other into their line of thinking.

"God, I could spend a whole lot more time here. This is fabulous." Aiden had a moment of shock as he said it almost to himself. She knew it was partially because of how beautiful the gardens were. But Kelly knew, deep inside, that she was also part of that reason. Because she was feeling it too.

What was this growing between them? They'd only just met yesterday. Why did it feel like she'd known him for much, much longer? And why was she already feeling a slight pain at the thought of it stopping too soon?

She linked her arm through his. The night wasn't over yet. "Come on; I think there's a blackberry cobbler with your name on it." She laid her head against his shoulder as they walked arm in arm back to her condo.

"Do you want ice cream with it? I have coconut, which is excellent if you like coconut. Or vanilla," she said as she peered into the freezer.

"Mmm, coconut, please. I don't know if I've ever had coconut ice cream."

"You're going to love this stuff. It's my weakness. I found this at the little market down the street. It's produced by a specialty company here in Portland. Natural. Totally healthy and good for you." She snickered as he glanced up at her. "Hey, I figure I can read the ingredients, so it can't be all that bad."

He shrugged. "Works for me."

She added a scoop to both bowls, then put the ice cream back in the freezer.

Kelly led Aiden back out to the patio, over to the corner where she had a small living room laid out complete with loveseat and two chairs. She poured two glasses of water, then settled down on the bench next to Aiden.

"So what do you think?" She watched as he ate one bite, then another.

"Shhh. You're interrupting my love affair over here."

"That good, huh? I can leave you two alone."

"No way. I need you to get me a second bowl when I'm done."

"And that would be now?" She asked as she watched him lick the last of the blackberries off of his spoon. Mesmerized by every movement he made.

He handed her his bowl. "Same thing?" He grinned. "I just don't get food like this out at sea. This has to last me a long while, until I get back to civilization."

Kelly walked back into the kitchen, scooped up another helping, added the ice cream, returned to her spot on the couch.

They finished in silence, enjoying every last bite.

"I love summertime." She sighed.

"Me too."

Kelly glanced over, looking at every line on his face. Her eyes danced from his eyes to his lips, and back again. She'd met him twenty-four hours before. And already she couldn't imagine him not being here, a part of her life.

He was so comfortable, in a good way. They already clicked. They had fallen into patterns. She could see him contemplating much the same thing as he glanced back at her.

"Weird, huh?"

"Yeah."

"Kelly, I ..." They moved so quickly; she wondered later who made the first move.

His hands moved around her neck, pulling her into him. His lips found hers, crashing into a kiss that made them both catch their breath.

She placed her hand on the cushion between them, stopping her world from spinning.

In some ways, she'd thought this feeling was lost to her, forever.

Yet this is what she'd missed, oh, so much.

The hardness of a male body. The musky scent that followed as she trailed from his face, down past his ear, down.

THE WRITER

She ran her hands over his chest. Feeling every muscle.

She wanted more than feeling; she wanted to see every inch of him. To see him in all his glory. To touch every inch of what made him male.

She let her hands run free. They slid up his arms, over the stubble on his face, until she settled in his hair. A warmth like no other poured over her.

She missed touching someone else, deeply, beyond the hug of a daughter, brother or friend. She missed touching someone intimately. The tingle that came from finding the perfect spots.

As she moved, as she touched, she felt him react. She felt him explore too.

And Aiden knew what he was doing.

His eyes said he wanted all that she was offering. He understood what she needed. He saw her sensuality, her holdbacks, her reservations, her desire.

His eyes blazed as he took in her femaleness, in a way that said he hadn't done that in a while. He moved expertly, yet in a way that said he hadn't been there in a very long time.

They stopped for just a moment, a look passing between them that said they understood. They understood where they were, now, in the moment.

They both had been through so much. They both had faced the worst and were in the process of bouncing back. Both had been a part of something deep, a marriage that they enjoyed, never doubted until the end came. To look forward was hard. Yet both were willing to try, right here in the present.

That was then; this was now.

And now, with someone new, it felt different, unique, animated, on fire. They were ready. And they wanted to explore.

With each other.

Kelly lingered under his touch, enjoying the feeling of being alive again.

Alive was a very good thing indeed.

Without thinking, only feeling, Aiden let his hands roam, navigating as if he'd been there many times. Yet with a question jumping from his eyes that said, "Is this okay?"

Her hands found his chest, scrunched his shirt as if holding on for dear life.

Aiden deepened their kiss, tasting. Exploring the corners of her mouth, licking her lips, thoroughly savoring every inch of her. The more he kissed her, every movement he made, she mirrored him. They fit together as if they had done this a thousand times before.

Kelly wanted this, needed this. She'd had no idea how just how badly until this very moment. It made her feel human again. Like a person who had a life, who had a future. She knew she couldn't get this from holding onto the past. From holding on to a memory that was no longer her world.

So she explored something that was so new, yet so familiar at the same time.

She moved her hands over his body, never breaking their connection. They went deeper, tongues tangling. Again. And again.

His hands gently moved up her thigh, under her dress. He skimmed his fingers around lace. Touching. Teasing.

He continued roaming, finding the swell of her breasts. He moaned. "Kelly ..." His lips traced a trail down her neck, onto her collarbone, while his fingers settled on lightly flicking her nipples through the fabric.

She shivered at his touch.

Kelly dropped her forehead to his, eyes closed. Relishing the feeling growing between them. And so much more.

"Aiden ..." She felt the roughness of his beard against her skin. Moved her hands along his collar, down to the first button.

One. Two. Then another. Let her hands roam over his chest. Felt every muscle, every inch.

He reached for her zipper, moved his hands to unclasp her bra. Cupped her breasts. Teased her with the pads of his thumbs.

"Aiden." She rose. Grabbed his hands and pulled him up. "Not out here."

He followed her through the door, watched and followed as she made her way down the hall.

She turned, folded into him once more. He dropped lower to match her height, cupped her ass and lifted, aligning them perfectly together. She encircled his waist with her legs.

She melted into him. Faded into him as she drowned in his heat.

More. She wanted more. As much as he could give. As much as they could share.

He moved to the bed, let her slide down his thigh until she was in front of him.

She moved, grabbed his hands, fell back, taking him with her.

And in a flurry, clothes flew until they were skin to skin, touch to touch.

Nothing between them. Nothing to hide behind.

Only the chance to explore.

She traced her fingers down over his chest, his stomach. Touched his arms. Linked their fingers. Kissed him again and again.

He moved down. Flicked his tongue over her nipples as she arched into him.

Like an ocean's waves, she felt it build. She saw it there on the horizon, coming closer and closer. She hadn't thought much about it in months. Yet there it was, coming closer. She took pleasure in it, called to it.

And with everything he did, he returned to her. His eyes saw everything. She saw them shine, share with her, his passion, his emotion, his nervousness.

She let it flow back into him. *I get it. I'm there too.*

She knew this was so right.

Still. The slight subconscious worry was there. Tom. Michelle. They understood it. They accepted it. They worked through it.

We can be here. We *should* be here. It's okay. It's time. It's where we need to be. It's the right time for this, for us.

Kelly guided his hands where she needed them most.

Touch me there. And there.

She was where she wanted to be. And it was the scariest, most wonderful place on earth.

She needed this, wanted this. Now.

She asked. He gave. She explored. He sighed.

They continued the journey, together, every inch.

She touched him. Felt him quiver. Gently pulled him in. Listened to his needs. Gave unconditionally.

Then they rode it, just the two of them. A feeling like no other.

In that instant, they knew.

They lay together, front to front, forehead to forehead. Eye to eye. Heart to heart.

"I've got to go." He looked at his watch, knew he was in trouble. "I really gotta go."

THE WRITER

Kelly hugged him close. "We'll figure this out, right?" She was afraid to let him go.

"We will. I promise."

"I'll drive you."

"No. You don't have to."

"Yes, it's easy for me. I can get you back quicker. I'm in the garage, downstairs. I'm fine."

"Okay."

They rode down together. Got into her car. Drove back to the water, to the docks, where she would let him go.

He turned to her. Kissed her. "Kelly, I'll be in touch, somehow. Calling, texting, it's all difficult. Email's easiest. We can start with that. I'm out for the next few months."

"Okay. I'll take your lead. You know where I am." She kissed him. Looked into his eyes. Memorizing this, now, for later.

"Bye."

She watched him walk out, back to the ship, out of Portland. Out of her life. For now.

Chapter Seven

Kelly opened her eyes, glancing over at the pillow lying beside her. She smiled. Just a few hours earlier, he'd been lying there next to her.

She could still smell him. She could still see him, with his sleepy eyes and dimple.

He had her so charged up.

Kelly hugged the pillow close, relishing in the afterglow of one of the best nights in recent memory.

Okay, maybe Beth had been right. Maybe it was time to get back to living, find something worth living for. Besides work.

For the first time in months, she imagined a man in her life again. And while before she always envisioned life to be with Tom, her husband of twenty-five years, for the first time she could see a spot in her life for someone else.

She rose, made a cup of tea, and headed out to her balcony to overlook the city once again. Though she couldn't see it, she knew Aiden's ship was just off in the distance. That he was there, working, getting ready to leave port later tonight.

Was he thinking of her?

Kelly admitted to herself that even if it had been a one night stand, it had been a great one. She'd take it and move on. Because now she knew she really could move on. As long as she found someone that matched her spirit. Like Tom. Like Aiden.

In the midst of her daydreams, she heard her phone beep. Grabbing it, she expected her daughter. To her surprise, it was a new number, added two nights before. Aiden.

Hi. Just wanted to say hi. I enjoyed last night.

Kelly laughed. He was nervous. Just like she was. How do you text someone you've just met, don't have a dialog with yet? She thought for a moment. Thought about his moment of panic when he realized how late it was. Then typed.

Did you get reprimanded?

Yes ... It was worth it. :)

She laughed. Nodded her head. Yep, she couldn't agree more.

LOL. I would say sorry, but I wouldn't mean it. I enjoyed it too much.

Me too. Thanks isn't enough, but it'll have to do for now. For dinner. For everything.

Accepted. And now you owe me. :)

THE WRITER

Soon. Promise. I'll think of something.

Kelly felt her breath catch. Did that mean he was thinking there would be more to this? She'd have to think about that.

Not that she'd mind. She really enjoyed him. She loved his laughter, his opinions. She loved the way they spoke together, the way they seemed to click right from the beginning.

She knew that didn't come easily; that was something you either had or didn't. You either matched styles immediately, or you wouldn't have that rapport. She'd had it with Tom. She felt it with Aiden. From the moment he sat down next to her, they seemed to hum together on the same wavelength. Understanding each other's ways almost from the beginning.

Kelly knew he'd be busy. She knew he was leaving. Time to get back to normal, everyday life, right here in Portland.

She tidied up her kitchen. Grabbed a quick shower and got ready for her day.

She set up her office on her balcony, laptop front and center with a glass of ice tea alongside. She opened up her latest book, started working on the chapter she'd been stuck on just two days before.

She saw her characters in a whole new way, and let the words spill out onto the page. Kelly read through it, tears forming in her eyes. *Great finish.*

She thought of Aiden. *Great inspiration.*

She edited. She changed a few words. She read it again. And with a deep sigh, hit save. She needed a break.

Stretching, she reached for her phone. Another text from Aiden.

Hey, what are you doing?

Kelly's heart skipped a beat. She quickly texted back.

At home, writing.

Come to the ship. Last day here. I can't leave – punished. :) But you could come.

Really?

Yes

Okay

Go to the front of the tour line. Talk to the guys at the table. They'll get you on.

K. Give me 30 minutes or so.

See you soon.

Flustered, happy, excited, Kelly danced into her office, stowing her computer. She changed clothes, added a touch of lip gloss, grabbed her purse and headed for the door.

Forty minutes later, she passed the long line of people waiting for the tour and approached the check-in table. She waited for movement, then leaned in.

"Excuse me; Captain Maddock said to check in with you about having someone bring me on board?"

The young man sitting at the table signaled to a man standing off to the side. He approached.

"Hello, Ms. Sorenson. I'm Lieutenant Stevenson. Please follow me."

THE WRITER

He took a side bridge, bypassing the other civilians waiting to board the ship for the tour. He brought her to a deck, left her waiting in the shade. "Wait here, Ms. Sorenson, Captain Maddock will be right out." He turned and made his way down the stairs.

Kelly moved to the side, watched as a tour group passed by. She listened in as the guide began describing some of the duties on this part of the ship.

She glanced around, wondering what this life would be like. It was so unfamiliar to her. She had so many questions. Where would she begin, if she had the chance, to find out more about his life? How could she understand something that was so new, when she knew he'd be sailing again in a matter of hours?

She thought about Aiden, how much she'd enjoyed their back-and-forth banter from the moment they met. How in sync they were with the words they spoke, the moves they made. How in a matter of moments, they'd developed something that took some people a lifetime to find.

She hadn't realized how much she missed the little things she'd always taken for granted.

The closeness. The touch. The gentle connection that made individuals a couple.

As much as she hadn't admitted it herself, hadn't even thought about before this weekend, she knew it was the one thing that could make her fall quickly all over again.

And then, he was there. Standing next to her, looking more handsome than she had remembered. Dressed in his full white uniform, hat tipped just so. He took her breath away.

They eyed each other with sideways glances. A hint of a smile touched each of their lips.

His knuckles brushed hers as he leaned closer. Yet she knew, here, in this location, respectability was imperative. She waited for him to take the lead.

"Thanks for coming." His eyes said he was happy to see her. They also said he wanted much more than to see her standing there beside him.

Kelly responded, breathless. "I couldn't get here fast enough." She watched as he almost fell apart right there, on the deck.

"Come with me." Aiden turned and motioned her down the stairs.

Down in the hallway, he bypassed her, leading her into its depths. He saluted personnel as they passed by.

He stopped. Looked behind her. Unlocked a door and pushed her in, quickly shutting the door behind them.

Aiden swung her around, pushing her against the door. He threw his hat off to the side, placed both hands gently on her cheeks.

He moved inches from her. Searching her eyes for some hidden reason they were driving each other crazy.

She could feel his breath. She could taste his lips against hers. She leaned in, wanting more.

He searched her face before letting himself go. "That was the hardest thing I've ever had to do. Professionalism sucks."

Every inch of her body tingled, heated as his lips crashed into hers, taking her all in.

Kelly let herself be consumed by his kiss. She traced his bottom lip with her tongue, nibbled at the corner of his mouth.

She heard herself moan as she felt the soft pads of his fingers gently caress behind her ears, down the back of her neck.

She fisted his shirt, allowing herself to run her hands up against his perfect body.

THE WRITER

Aiden pulled away, resting his forehead against hers. "You drive me crazy." His hands moved down, molded to her lower back. "I wish we had more time."

"We're going to have to get creative." Kelly suddenly saw the weeks and months ahead playing out before her eyes. She breathed him in as she moved her hands under his shirt.

Was this insane? She knew it was. Yet she knew she would take all she could get. She'd learned the hard way that every day mattered. So she was willing to take things one day at a time. Live each day to its fullest. And right now it told her to enjoy fully this man standing in front of her.

Nothing before her had ever felt so right. She hadn't expected this. Didn't go searching for this. Yet here it was, here *he* was.

He was flesh and blood. With as much pain and hurt in his history as hers. He got that. He'd lived it and bounced back from it too.

And in a move as old as time itself, they'd found each other. Found the one thing that gave each of them hope they'd be okay once again.

She was awash in feeling, wished it could last forever. Even though the realist told her, it would come to an end way too soon.

"I want you so much." She wanted him more than anything she'd wanted in her life.

Five little words released a tidal wave of emotions.

Aiden could no longer control anything inside him. He lifted her skirt, shimmied it up in his hand. Glided the other up her thigh, reaching, reaching ...

He stopped. Eyes burning with hunger, he pulled away, raising an eyebrow. "No underwear?"

She laughed at the look in his eyes. "Figured they'd get in the way."

His forehead grazed hers; he kissed her nose. "You're killing me."

And just like that, he was there. Touching her tenderly in a perfect way. Letting his eyes say what words couldn't. Pushing a lock of hair behind her ear as he nibbled. Matching her movements in every way.

They spoke without words, promised with only an embrace.

Kelly watched every move he made. Memorizing his taste, his touch, his manner.

Eyes together, he slipped in, enveloped by the warmth of each other. How could anything feel so good, so right? She'd never imagined it was possible, ever again. And yet, here he was, here they were. Together.

He moved quickly, knowing their time together was short. But neither of them needed time. They were energized, revitalized by the knowledge that they had one more chance with each other.

Because of one split decision, they had met. They had a chance.

They could feel it with every move they made.

Higher, higher, she felt the temperature rise. He touched her in ways she hadn't thought were possible, ever again.

Bliss. Pure ecstasy.

They fell.

And fell.

And found themselves in each other's arms.

This was the start of something good. They knew it. They could feel it.

But for now, they'd have to let go.

THE WRITER

They caught their breath. He leaned in, kissed her gently. "I'm sorry, but we have to go."

"I know."

Kelly stepped into his bathroom to look in the mirror. She straightened her skirt, put her hair back in a clip. With a touch of lip gloss, she felt presentable once again.

She moved back into his bedroom, his living quarters for his time at sea. She took it all in, memorizing the walls, his bed, his book shelf, imagining him living there day to day.

Her eyes stopped on his, smiling back at her. He reached out, pulled her to him. "You know this is crazy, right?"

"Totally." Two days ago she never would have believed any of this was possible. Now, she couldn't imagine her life without him in it.

"It's going to be difficult at best."

"Who said anything worth having isn't difficult? It's worth the effort." She'd learned that in the hardest way possible.

"You don't know what it's like, me being at sea for weeks and weeks."

"I guess I'll learn." She was willing to move this forward, to find out what this was between them.

"I can email you. It's the best way we can talk."

"I'm a good writer." She grinned, knowing full well what she was capable of.

He laughed. "I'm sure you are."

"You'll love what I have to say."

"I can't wait."

"So we're going to do this. We're going to make this work?"

"Looks that way."

"I'm going to miss you."

"I'm going to miss you too."

Aiden lifted his hand, traced a finger down her cheek, tucked a strand of hair behind her ear. He memorized every movement she made, every inch of her face.

"I gotta get you out of here."

"Lead the way."

He opened the door, peered to the left and the right. He grabbed her hand and tugged, locked the door behind him.

As he made his way down the corridor, to the bridge, they ran into Mike. "Captain." Mike saluted his friend with a smirk on his face as his eyes roamed from Kelly back to his friend. Aiden responded with a friendly punch in the arm.

"You remember Kelly?"

Mike held out his hand. "Hi, Kelly, nice to see you again. Getting the VIP tour?" He choked back a laugh as a scowl crossed Aiden's face.

"Nice to see you again, Mike. I wanted to thank you for dinner the other night. And the wine. And dessert." She snickered as Mike's smile dimmed, remembering how much dinner had truly cost him.

Aiden laughed, clearly happy she had gotten the better of his friend.

"Yeah, yeah." Mike glanced at Aiden, with mild irritation. Then burst out laughing. "Okay, I probably deserved that."

"Ya think?" Aiden grinned.

"Okay, gotta go. I'll let you two get back to whatever you were doing. Oh," Mike's eyes held Aiden's for a moment. "Sorry, but the meeting's still on in Donavon's office in an hour."

"Thanks."

"Nice to see you again, Kelly. Bye."

They watched him turn a corner, then continued walking towards the stairs.

THE WRITER

"I like him." Kelly hadn't spent a lot of time with Mike, but what she'd seen in his eyes told her he was fiercely loyal to his friend. She knew he had Aiden's back, could see it in the way they played. Somehow she knew he'd been there through it all.

"Yeah, he's all right." She knew he was playing it down.

They made their way back on deck, with Aiden showing her a few of the features of the ship as they passed by. And with a couple of turns, she was back on deck, back by the stairs that would lead off the ship.

"I really have to go. I just really wanted to see you again. Honestly, I didn't mean to take you into my room ..." Aiden stood close, memorizing everything about her face.

Kelly placed a finger over his lips. "Two participants and all." She moved in just a little closer. "I'm glad you invited me. I was thinking about you."

She grazed her fingers over his, careful not to bring attention to her movements. "You know, there's a ton of reasons why we're not meant to work, why this entire thing we've started here is crazy. Why we should leave this all right here and call it what it is: a really good one night stand. But I can't. I'm smitten." Her eyes danced as she took him in.

She had no idea what this was or where it would end up, but she was having more fun than she'd had in a very long time. It felt good to be looked at, touched, the way Aiden had touched her in the past forty-eight hours.

He raised an eyebrow. "Smitten? Do people talk that way?"

She laughed. "They do if they're romance writers."

Aiden chuckled as he moved in as close as he dared.

"You've definitely captured my attention." He grew serious. "This wasn't a one night stand. Not for me. It's there for me."

"It's there for me too."

While the rest of the world moved around them, they stood, staring. Absorbing. Memorizing.

A passing tourist group brought them back to reality. They stepped aside while people moved by.

"I'm not sure how this is going to work. We'll take it one day at a time."

Kelly nodded. "We'll figure it out. If I've learned anything over the past eighteen months, it's that life is short. This is where I want to be, right now."

"Me too." He held her gaze, engraining upon her that he meant it. "I'll write."

"Me too." She gave him a wicked smile.

He brushed his lips over hers, knew it was the best he could do given the circumstances. "Bye."

"Bye."

With a flick of his wrist, Lieutenant Stevenson appeared once again. She followed him off the ship.

Chapter Eight

Aiden sat down in a corner of the cafeteria planning to inhale his food as fast as possible to avoid the barrage of incoming questions he knew he'd have to answer. Mike had been in hot pursuit all day. They'd been too busy to talk. But that wouldn't last forever. Eventually, they'd be face to face, and the questioning would begin.

Not that he didn't want to tell him it had been the very best weekend of his life in a very long time. He just wanted to keep it all to himself for as long as possible.

A forkful of this and a spoonful of that and he'd almost made it ...

"Hey, you've been avoiding me." Mike shoulder bumped him as he took the seat beside him.

"I haven't," though Aiden avoided his eyes.

A shoulder bump again. He couldn't do it forever. He looked up. "What?"

"What? You have to ask what? How'd it go? Was Saturday night good? It must have been since she was on the boat yesterday. Talk."

"It was good."

Mike coughed out a laugh in between bites.

"Good? Really? That's not going to work here. We're not like college buddies here counting our conquests. This is different. This is the first time you've been out with someone. And from the look of things, it went well. *Talk.*" Mike wouldn't let him go that easy.

"We had a good night." Aiden wasn't going to make this easy. He didn't want to share. He knew Mike meant well, but he was still trying to put all the pieces together himself.

"Okay, I can see you're going to make this difficult. Let's get passed this *good* crap. You liked her. Is there more to it than this weekend? Or was it just a very nice weekend?" Mike looked expectantly at his friend.

A whoosh of breath and he fell back against his chair. Aiden scrubbed a hand over his face. "More. I think there's more."

"You think, or you know?"

"I don't know," Aiden said a little gruffer than he'd intended. "I mean, I do know. Yes, there's more. We're going to email, get to know each other. We'll see from there."

"Wow. Who would have guessed?" Mike said as much to himself as he did to Aiden. He leaned in, trying to catch his friend's eyes. And with one look, he saw all he needed to see.

"Hey, I'm happy for you. I mean that." He tapped his friend on the shoulder.

Aiden leaned forward, braced his elbows on the table and laid his head in his hands. "This is crazy, right? I mean, what the hell am I doing? I've never even dated since Michelle. And here I am, totally infatuated with someone I met barely two days ago. Crazy, right?"

Aiden had thought about it all day. He knew it was insane even to think this had potential. He'd be at sea for weeks. She was a thousand miles from his home. They couldn't start a relationship like this. Could they? He'd gone back and forth with this conversation in his head for hours. He'd had fun, enjoyed her more than he'd imagined he could with someone new. But under these circumstances? What were the chances? He looked expectantly back at Mike.

"I think you're overthinking this. What do you want out of this?"

That was the thing. He really didn't know. "I have no idea."

Mike continued, "A one night stand? A wife? Something in between?"

Aiden looked startled as he fell back in his chair once more. With a hint of anger, he replied, "Now you're just pissing me off. Why the hell would I want a wife?"

"Okay, so we ruled that out."

"Obviously."

"A one night stand?"

"No. I mean, it would be great if that's all it turns out to be. But I would love to see her again. I really enjoyed being with her."

"Okay then. There's your answer. Quit thinking about it. Email her. Take it one day at a time. See where it leads. You'll be back in September, meet up again and see what happens."

That seemed easy enough.

Mike brought his finger up to his face leaned in and caught Aiden's eye. "Look, I'm not an expert here. I've been married forever. And I honestly never want to be in your position. But I've seen you change a lot in these past eighteen months. I know you haven't dated. But it hasn't been a lack of potential. Remember Jennifer at the party before we left? She had her eye on you from the moment we got there."

Aiden's eyes started rolling at the thought. "Shit, no. She's had her hooks on every single guy on base. No."

Mike continued, "That's what I'm getting at. If you wanted a one night stand, it wouldn't have been any easier than her."

"No."

Mike changed direction. "Okay, what about that thing over at Steve's house last spring. You sat with his sister, what was her name?"

"Amy."

"That's right, Amy. She was coming on to you big time. We all could see it."

Once again, Aiden shook his head, rolled his eyes. "No. She wasn't my type at all. We talked a little, but I didn't have an interest."

"See? You might not have dated anyone. But you've looked."

Aiden sat there thinking about what his friend said. He hadn't dated. He hadn't wanted to. The whole process seemed way out of his comfort zone. He'd always had thoughts of Michelle in his mind, hadn't wanted to cross that bridge. The women he met, none of them had done anything to him, no flicker, no twist, no buzz, no tingle. Until Kelly.

"I never thought about it. I've never met anyone I'd even ask. I've never wanted to. I've never felt ready to do anything; to move forward."

"So what was different this weekend? I saw you glaring at me when I said yes to Beth's invitation to join them for dinner. But you sure changed your tune when you sat next to Kelly. A couple of minutes in, Beth and I could both tell you guys were enjoying each other."

"She's funny. She's interesting. She ... I don't know," Aiden fell back in his chair once again, searching his friend for help. "I haven't done this since college."

"I know."

"How am I supposed to know what to do?" Aiden said it a little softer than he'd intended. He could feel the catch in his throat, didn't want it to show.

It did. Mike picked it up. But continued as if he didn't. "Well, I don't know the whole story, but it seems to me you did pretty well this weekend."

Mike smirked at the look his friend gave him.

"Aiden, look, nobody says there's a perfect way to do this. There aren't any rules. I haven't done this in eons myself. And no offense, I never want to. But you are where you are. You met. You connected. What are the odds? And I can tell you connected; it's all over your face." Mike shouldered his friend once again.

Aiden smiled. "Okay, okay. We *connected.*" His smile tumbled into a full-fledged grin. "Very well."

Mike reached out to fist bump his friend. "Nothing can be bad if you *connected.*"

Aiden turned serious. "Did you know her husband died a week before Michelle?"

"Yeah, Beth mentioned it. We got our dinners to go; ate them outside at a park nearby and talked for a while."

"It was strange. The coincidences kept adding up. But it was more than that. It was like they all spun together, almost as if we'd been living parallel lives up until this point. We have a lot in common. We have the same humor. A lot of the same interests and beliefs. It all happened so fast."

"That's a good thing, right?"

"Yeah, I know it is. I'm old enough to know what I don't want. But this threw me off guard. She did something to me. I didn't expect it. And it's not like I'm going to see her again anytime soon. Not until September at least. So who knows what'll happen between now and then, if anything."

"But you want something to happen." Mike could see it was true without asking.

Aiden nodded. "Yeah, I do. That's crazy, right? I mean, Portland, come on. Even when we get back to San Diego, it's going to be hard. What am I thinking?" He scrubbed a hand over his face, talking with himself more than speaking with his friend.

Mike bumped him to break his train of thought. "Look, I'm going to say it again. I think you're putting too much into this. You had a great weekend, right?"

"Right."

"And you wouldn't mind if it continued, right?"

"Right."

"So what's next?"

"We agreed to email each other. You know it's the best way. Plus, she's a writer," Aiden smiled.

Mike smirked back. "I heard that too. You know how to pick 'em. A romance writer?" He raised an eyebrow at his friend.

"A very good romance writer. Or at least that's what she led me to believe. She showed me several of her books."

"Beth told me she's great. Award-winning as a matter of fact. She keynotes and speaks all over the country. Her books are in multiple languages. I'd say she's pretty good."

Aiden gave Mike a sheepish look. Covered his face as he whispered. "I might have downloaded her books before we left."

THE WRITER

Mike cackled. "I would have been disappointed if you hadn't. Just don't let anyone see you read them. I'll hold your secret, but the rest of the guys? Shit. Trouble. That's all I'm going to say."

"Don't worry; nobody's getting my Kindle." He'd probably just leave it in his room. Why take a chance on one of the guys stealing it to find out what he was reading. It's not like he'd ever had his Kindle in his hands before. There'd be questions if he started now.

Mike broke Aiden's train of thought.

"So email her already."

"Yeah?"

"Yes. Just do it. See where it goes."

Aiden breathed in a deep breath as if the world had lifted from his shoulders. He didn't need Mike's permission to move forward. But somehow it made him feel better knowing he had his support.

A simple email. What would be the harm in that?

And if it led to something more? All the better.

Chapter Nine

"Hey, you got five minutes?" Kelly needed a sounding board, and she knew just the man for the job.

Chris Nolan took his job of big brother very seriously. A mere ten months older than Kelly, they'd been almost inseparable since birth. Wherever Chris went, Kelly followed. Growing up, they played the same sports, hung out with the same friends. Double dated in high school, graduated from the same college. Even after they were married, they called each other regularly, confiding just about everything that crossed their minds.

"Sure, what's up?" Chris was on rounds at the hospital, checking in with patients that had been admitted the night before. As a cardio specialist, he often spent several hours at the hospital before heading into the office for his daily appointments. Kelly knew his hours well and usually managed to catch him when he could sneak in a few minutes.

"Um ..." She wasn't quite sure how to begin. He'd helped her over so many hurdles these past eighteen months; she simply couldn't imagine not telling him her news. Yet how to say it was something entirely different.

"Baby, you okay?" With all the issues in the past couple of years, he didn't like it when he heard uncertainty in her voice.

She hemmed and hawed. Thought. Then blurted out, "I had sex this weekend."

There. That's ripping the band-aid off and getting straight to the point. Kelly covered her face with her other hand. "Sorry, TMI, right?"

"No. No. Not at all. I mean, wow. Really? You okay?" Chris stammered, not sure what to say. "Who? How? Okay, I don't really mean how, but ... Really?" He went into his office and shut the door, sitting down behind his desk.

Kelly laughed. "You sound even more confused than I feel."

"Well, I have to admit, that's the last thing I expected coming from you. Did you even have a date this weekend?" He didn't recall her saying anything.

"No. Not really. Well, kind of." She'd always blurted her stories out when she had something to say. Knowing she was on a time crunch, she gave him the thirty-second version.

"Beth called ... Dinner ... Two Navy guys ... We hit it off ... He walked me home ... I invited him for dinner ... And, well, dessert turned into *dessert*. And the ship sailed this morning." She let out a sigh as if she'd been talking for hours.

"Wow."

"I know, right?"

"So now what?" Chris was trying to bounce back from shock fast. He'd known this day was coming, but he'd assumed he'd have some warning.

THE WRITER

"That's why I'm calling you. I need to process. I mean, this is good, right?"

"Of course, it's good. You sound happy, minus all the confusion I hear." He chuckled. "I think it's great. You need to live again. And if this happened this weekend, it means you're ready. No regrets, right?"

"No. None, actually. I mean, if this just turns out to be a one-night stand, it was a great one night stand."

"You're sure you're okay with that? Because honestly, he's Navy. They go in and out of ports all the time. I'm not saying that to upset you. And hell, I don't know anything about him. But one night stands can't be any easier, knowing your ship is sailing in a few days." Chris hated to burst her bubble, but he wanted her to have a reality check too.

"I guess I didn't mention that part. Aiden's wife died eighteen months ago. Of cancer. December second."

Chris felt the wind knock out of him. "Fuck."

"Strange, right?

"Very."

"The coincidences just kept piling up."

"Well, I can see why you two connected so quickly. But was it more a grief thing? I guess you might not even know." He knew grief did strange things.

"I've been asking myself that. I honestly can't answer it. I will say that we didn't talk a whole lot about Michelle, his wife, and Tom. Of course, they were there, sort of. But we talked about a lot of things. Our kids. Our interests. Even some of our plans for the future. We cooked dinner together, talked about places we've been. I mean normal date stuff. We had fun. We definitely connected."

"You had *dessert*; I hope you connected."

Kelly giggled. She could see the look on her brother's face. "Sorry, big brother. I'm sure I've given you way too much to think about for the rest of today." Of course, she wasn't sorry at all. Just saying it all out loud made her feel better, put things more into perspective.

"I just don't know what I want out of this. I don't know where I want this to go, if any place at all. Is that wrong?"

"Baby, if he put a smile on your face, he's the best."

"Really?"

"Really. One step at a time. Don't put too much pressure on this. Be grateful for the weekend. And if it turns into something more, then run with it."

"So it's okay either way? I mean, I don't want to seem too dependent, that I run after the first guy I hook up with."

"Give me a break; no one will accuse you of that."

"Yeah, but I don't want it to seem like that. Yikes, now I'm just bullshitting here, aren't I? I've confused myself. I'm throwing things out from every which way. But it's all because I don't know what to think. This means I've stepped over to the next phase. And as much as I'm okay with that, I also feel a little bad about it."

"Stop. Don't say that. It's been eighteen months. It's okay."

"It's okay," she repeated, trying to convince herself.

"This is a huge step. You did it. You're moving forward, and that's a good thing. One step at a time. Just see where it goes from here."

Kelly chewed on her lip. So much of her said she was okay with this. She'd enjoyed the weekend. She'd enjoyed Aiden. And then she opened her phone and found a photo of Tom. She felt like a ping pong ball, floating back and forth between feelings.

THE WRITER

Eighteen months was a long time to live without someone. She'd missed Tom. But after this weekend, she admitted she'd missed something even more. Intimacy. She'd had no idea how much. Until she touched Aiden.

"Chris?"

"Yes?"

"This is a good thing, right? I mean, Tom ..." she contemplated what this meant.

"Baby, stop. It's fine. You know Tom would be more than all right with it. He'd want you to be happy. He'd want you to be whole again. Have a life."

"I know. We'd talked about it even. But it just seems so different now that I'm here, that I've done this. It's like the old life is gone. I'm moving on. That's okay, right?" Her voice grew quiet.

"You know it is." He waited for her to respond.

"I know. It's just it nags at me. You know?"

"I can imagine. But coming from me, the one who knows you better than anyone, I give you full permission to run with this, all right? I know you don't need it. I know you know. But still, it's all perfectly normal. You're fifty-three. You deserve to be happy. And a little *dessert* now and then can definitely do the trick." He snickered as he said it.

"Creep," she said affectionately. She truly loved him, was grateful for him always being there for her.

"You know it. Gotta go."

"Thanks."

"Anytime."

Chapter Ten

From: Aiden
Subject: Hi
To: Kelly

Hi.

I said I would connect, get the ball rolling. So here we go.

You're going to figure out quickly that I'm not a writer. Even my daughters don't expect much. I don't spend much time at the computer writing, usually just checking in with the programs I use every day. If I write, it's a report. Only the things I absolutely have to do. So this should be interesting.

I'm not really sure where to begin.

I've been thinking about you. I miss you. Thanks again for dinner, it gets me through some of these awful meals we have on board. Trust me when I say you're much better dinner companion than Mike and the crew.

You have my email now. Looking forward to getting to know you better.

Aiden

Chapter Eleven

From: Kelly
Subject: Let's get started
To: Aiden

Aiden. Aiden. Aiden. You're about to find out I write even more than I talk. That's saying a lot, right?

I know email's going to be a little bit more challenging than being able to talk or actually see each other. But there's no reason we can't have fun with this. So let's learn more about each other a little at a time by playing a game.

It's called Q&A. Easy enough.

I'll ask a question; you give me your answer. Just one per email. Then at the end, give me your question, and I'll send my answer.

LORI OSTERBERG

Easy, peasy.

I know you'll get the hang of it. (Wink, wink)

And let's make it interesting. No repeating questions. In other words, you can't ask me the same question I ask you. And you have to give a story with your answer, something personal, that helps us get to know each other better.

My game. I go first.

What makes your mom and dad special?

Kelly

Chapter Twelve

From: Aiden
Subject: Mom and dad
To: Kelly

Sounds like a good game. I'll play.

Mom and Dad, huh? Okay, I can do that.

I was born in Maryland. Navy brat. We traveled a bit when I was little, but we ended up back in Maryland when I was twelve and stayed there through high school. They still live there today.

I went to the Naval Academy, followed in my Dad's footsteps. My older brother took the same route. He's in Washington DC now, still in the Navy too.

What makes my Mom special? The way she loved us, no matter what. She wouldn't have any of it when we thought we got too big for hugs and kisses. She'd just do it anyway. You always know she loves you; you'll never forget it because she's always there, always tells you. She would reprimand us, punish us, correct us. But at the end of the day, she'd always come into our rooms and give us a hug and say "Love you more than ever." That was her thing, still is when I call her. She was my rock when Michelle died. She stayed with me for weeks. And every night would tell me she loved me more than ever. Even when I felt like complete shit and wanted to die. She'd say, "I know" and hug me tight and tell me she loved me more than ever.

My Dad? He was smart enough to pick Mom. He always told us to surround yourself with people smarter and better than you. And he'd always look at Mom and say she was the best; they didn't make them any better than her. He still says that too. He's been my role model all the way. Fair in every way. Strict when he had to be.

They're still the best. They're doing fine, travel a lot. They were everything I wanted my life to look like. Before.

Okay, a question from me. I don't even know, do you have sisters or brothers?

Aiden

Chapter Thirteen

From: Kelly
Subject: My brother Chris
To: Aiden

How beautiful, I love your Mom and Dad already. What amazing people, great role models. I'm glad you've had them as rocks in your life. It's so important to have them, isn't it?

For me, it was Christopher.

Chris is ten months older than me. Growing up, he used to introduce me as the oops baby because I was so close behind him. There was never a time when I was without him. I tagged along with him from the moment I could walk. If you look at photographs, it's the two of us. We were connected in so many ways.

When he started school, Mom always said I'd sit by the door and cry, waiting for him to come home. The happiest day of my life was when I got to go to school too; I got to be near him. We walked to school together. Sat at the kitchen table and did our homework together. Grew up together.

He played baseball, so I joined the softball team. He used *that* as a way to date all my friends on the team.

Ah, but that's a different story!

(I wasn't allowed to date anyone on the baseball team. They weren't good enough for me!)

Yeah, you gotta meet him. He's a character. Still is.

We graduated high school in San Jose, ended up going to Berkeley together. He met his wife Lisa there. I met Tom. Double dated. Both of us were married before we were twenty-five.

So that's the short of it. Now let me tell you who he is today.

Chris wanted to be a doctor from early on. He'd care for everyone in our neighborhood. Studied medical journals for the fun of it. Yeah, he was a sick kid.

But after college, he went to medical school, married Lisa in between it all. They waited a few years to have kids, but have two boys, Ian and Justin, that I adore. He's a heart specialist in San Francisco, loves what he does.

THE WRITER

We still talk at least once a day, even if it's just a quick text that says hello. Just knowing he's at the other end completes me somehow.

I first met Tom when we were college sophomores. But it wasn't love at first sight. We were in a psychology course together, were assigned to work on a project, just the two of us. He'd been crushing on me, so he used it as a way to spend time with me. He'd pretend not to understand something, asked if we could meet. So we'd meet for dinner, on the weekends. Yeah, you get it.

The first couple of weeks I found him kind of annoying. And I guess I mentioned it to Chris at one point. One kiss, however, and I figured out I really liked him too. That part never got relayed to Chris before he hunted him down and gave him the brotherly threat. Never really did find out what that was all about. But it gave us a laugh for years. "You remember the time you almost killed my future husband?"

Chris flew up and was in my condo four hours after I found out about Tom. He just grabbed me and hugged me. Sat on my couch and held me while I died. He didn't say a word because that's what great big brothers do. He was with me through it all, stayed two weeks after the funeral. And he flew up to be with me every couple of weeks after that.

He hit me upside the head a few times. Told me to cry it out, that it was okay. Made me scream one time at the top of my lungs, saying it was what I needed. Gave me permission to do very stupid things. Like, eat an entire half gallon of chocolate ice cream with a bottle of wine to chase it. Which I wouldn't recommend.

He doesn't judge, just holds my hand.

I called him Monday after you left Portland. I told him all about you. Yep, sorry, every detail. Well, maybe not every detail. Still, he got the picture.

He sat very quietly and listened. Then he said one thing.

"Baby, if he put a smile on your face, he's the best."

So that's how my big brother thinks of you.

He's right.

Okay, let's get down to the nitty-gritty. I wanna know all about your first date. Give me all the gushy details!

Kelly

Chapter Fourteen

From: Aiden
Subject: First date
To: Kelly

Thanks for introducing me to Chris. I feel like I know him already.

I was close to my older brother Alex growing up, though we don't see each other that much now. He's three years older, an admiral working at the Pentagon. He's married with two kids who are both married, no grandkids yet. We try and talk a couple of times a month, usually winds up being about mom and dad.

The nitty-gritty details of my first date, huh?

Not that exciting.

Homecoming, ninth grade. Several of us did dinner together, then the dance. Kind of hard to do much when your parents have to drive you wherever you go. Sue and I were a pretty hot item for the first half of the year. LOL. Did movies on the weekends. Went to school events together. I don't remember breaking up with her, just faded away I guess. Funny how things seemed so important to you then, now I can't even remember the details.

I met Michelle during sophomore year of college. She went to St Johns College, not too far from the Academy. I met her at a coffee shop one Saturday morning, which turned into a date that night. And we were inseparable from that point forward. Got married right out of college, we both graduated the same year.

You said you went to Berkeley, what's your degree in?

Aiden

Chapter Fifteen

From: Kelly
Subject: My degree
To: Aiden

Isn't it scary to think how young we were, diving into relationships, settling down?

I'm so glad the kids don't do that today. I remember having crushes at ten, twelve years old. Both my parents and grandparents started asking about the boys I was interested in from that point on. The assumption was you had someone in your life, especially once you got to high school.

Now we'd look at our kids like they were crazy if they settled down early. Taylor didn't even really date until college. She went to prom with a guy. They did large group "dates" if you can call them that. They just went out and had fun; never had the boyfriend/girlfriend drama we had. And yes, I'm counting my blessings on that one.

Berkeley. I changed my major three times before I graduated. Started out as an English major, which morphed into a psychology major. Then I finally settled in on a business marketing major with a minor in English. And somehow through it all, I still managed to graduate in four years.

Between my junior and senior year, I found an internship position for an advertising agency whose primary clients included newly forming tech companies in Silicon Valley. Now that was a ride.

That summer I'm pretty sure I worked twenty-four hours a day. But it was a blast. Of course, we were all twenty-somethings. We worked hard when we had to, and the benefits were fantastic. Benefits being parties! I learned a lot about marketing and advertising, made a ton of connections. I was very grateful for getting in on the ground level of that huge growth spurt; I know that's the reason I got my first job out of school, and why I moved easily into better positions.

I'd felt like I'd been doing that for a thousand years when we decided to move up to Portland. And that's when my English minor side came back into play. I'd taken a creative writing course, and always had the dream of writing a novel one day. I guess a lot of people have that dream, but I've kept it alive. I went to a couple of creative writing courses over the years, kept a list of possible book ideas close at hand.

THE WRITER

I wrote a couple of short stories a few years before we moved. I tried to sell them to no avail. But I never stopped trying. Or stopped writing.

I think the turning point was being able to do it full time. I approached it like a job. I went to work in the morning, made myself work full days. I wrote in the mornings, marketed in the afternoon. I knew how to make connections from my years at marketing and ad agencies, so I worked the system. I gave myself a goal of doing at least one thing every day that helped me push my work out there. And it worked.

I was scared to death that I would fall flat on my face, that it would end up being one very big hobby that never became self-sufficient. But I never lost faith that I had the potential to get it done. And I have to admit it all happened a lot faster than I thought it would. I think it kind of surprised everyone. It's been a wild ride, and I wouldn't change it for anything.

Okay, I know I made the rule, but I'm just curious, what did you major in? I'm not sure how the Naval Academy works and what majors are even available. Just curious, but not my question. :)

So being in the Navy, I'm sure you've been all over the world. You've probably lived in some pretty amazing places. What's been your favorite? Would you move there again if you could?

Kelly

Chapter Sixteen

From: Aiden
Subject: Best place I've lived
To: Kelly

The Academy offers more tech and engineering-related degrees. They have political science, some language programs. But for the most part it's all science based in tech and engineering. I have a computer engineering degree, which makes me a computer geek, I suppose. I was always the math and computer kid throughout school. Still like that stuff, give me science based things anytime over humanities. I'm not a writer, and can't live without spell check attached to my programs.

Believe it or not, I really haven't lived in that many places. I was born in Maryland. My parents moved to Hawaii when I was two and we stayed there for ten years. Then we moved back to Maryland. My dad eventually retired and they still live there today. After graduation, we married and spent our first few years there. Then I took a position in San Diego eighteen years ago and have been here ever since. Of course, I travel a lot for work. Luckily we could have some stability by living in the same place.

I guess I pretty much told you my feelings on snow the night we met. That's a big NO. Have no desire to live where it snows ever again. Visiting is one thing, living there is another.

Hawaii is beautiful, but I was so young, I really don't have a good perspective about living there. I've visited a few times, but I'm not sure I'm cut out for island living. I love the big city feel of San Diego. Always great weather. Access to the ocean, plus you can be just about anywhere quickly. I've never really considered leaving. We bought our house fifteen years ago with long term in mind. It's just a couple of blocks from the beach. We have great neighbors. A lot are military, a lot of retired as well. So it makes sense for me to stay there. At least that's always been my thought before.

I'm not sure now. Obviously, a lot has changed in my life. What will I do when I don't go back to the job? Does this place have what I want? I guess I'm taking things one day at a time.

Still young enough to change if I want to.

Your story got me thinking about changing things up. How you moved to start something new after your daughter went off to school. I like that idea. New place. New lifestyle. There's something to be said about that. And I really do love your condo's view. It made me think a bit more about a lock-and-leave kind

THE WRITER

of place. I had to hire help inside and out for when I'm out of town. That's tested my trust more than a few times.

Mike lives across the street, so his wife Janet checks in too. Michelle just always did everything. Now I have to make sure everything is well cared for when I'm gone. I guess I have to say I found a system that works. Still, the stress has been a bit much sometimes. I've had a couple of minor emergencies I had to have Janet deal with. Hard when you're not there.

So obviously the family house isn't a big deal to you, you chose to move on. So I'm a little intrigued; what do you think makes a house a home?

Aiden

CHAPTER SEVENTEEN

From: Kelly
Subject: A house a home
To: Aiden

Yep, you were stereotyped. Military in my mind means moving every few years. I had no idea your life could be so stationary, at least from a family perspective. I guess the Navy would be slightly different than other branches. Interesting.

We purchased our home in San Francisco two years before Taylor was born. Sold it when she was a sophomore in college. Can't believe we had it that long. But it was in a great neighborhood; we loved the community.

After Taylor left, we realized we had all of this space, and it was just the two of us. We started looking around for a smaller place, but took our time while thinking about what we wanted.

Tom's job opportunity came up before we'd made any decisions. We fell in love with Portland and thought it would be a great place to retire. So we jumped at the job offer, and it made our decision to sell that much easier.

We knew we didn't want yard work anymore, so that narrowed our focus. Tom's job was downtown, so purchasing something nearby made sense. We could eliminate a car.

Then came the downsizing process. Our house in San Francisco was thirty-five hundred square feet. My Portland condo is just under thirteen hundred square feet. So to say we sold off a bunch of stuff would be an understatement.

That process put a lot of things into perspective for me.

A number of years ago, Tom had a client that became an overnight millionaire. He flew to the top, had more money than he knew what to do with, and bought for the sake of buying. He loved his stuff. He had a very expensive car, a house quadruple the size of ours. His kitchen had all the latest gadgets. In fact, he had a couple of things that weren't even on the market yet; he "knew" people.

He and his wife had us over for dinner a few times. Each time we went on a grand tour, wandering through rooms to see their latest purchases. It was mindboggling. They had stuff everywhere. Their home theater, for example, had a DVD wall with thousands of movies. Knickknacks everywhere. They had an elevator to get to the second floor.

THE WRITER

I liked them; they were funny, warm-hearted people. They were always willing to jump in and help any way they could. They traveled, donated money at the drop of a hat. They were really good people.

But somewhere along the way their house became this place of stuff. And they were proud of their stuff. But to me, it all became one fancy show. They had everything, just to have it. They liked showing it off. They liked having it as a part of their checklist of things they'd acquired. Most of it had no meaning, other than the fact they could own it.

I have another friend that I run into occasionally at book fairs. She's a writer too. I've stayed with her a few times. She has traveled the world extensively. I'm sure there are very few places left unexplored. I've seen her passport; it's loaded.

She has a small, three bedroom ranch not far from the beach in a small town far away from a major city. She's lived there forever, and when you walk in, you would say it's very well loved. There's an old chair in the corner. A hodgepodge of artwork hanging on the wall. An old comforter thrown over the sofa.

But from the moment you enter, she starts telling you stories about everything in the room. You could be there weeks and not hear all the stories.

- A tribal leader gave her a mask hanging in the hallway.
- She donated some time in a small community, and they gave her a quilt.
- She met an artist on the beach and invested in her first piece of art.

The stories go on and on.

That, to me, is the difference between a house and a home. Anyone can have stuff. Anyone can buy a house. But it takes heart to turn a house into a home. You have to open yourself up to experiences. To trust. To love. And as you experience different things, they become your fondest memories.

You don't buy stuff just to have decor in your house. You hold onto something because of the meaning it gives to you. Your home is filled with things that you treasure.

You do that with personal things. And you can do that with memories. All of it adds up to make you who you are.

That's why it's easy to move to a new house. Because a house is just a house. It's the memories that matter most.

When I look back, I've had some of the most breathtaking experiences. They've made me into the person I am today. I wouldn't trade those for anything. What you see in my home is a reflection of that time, that space, those memories. They remind me of each moment and what it's so very precious to me.

One of the best days of my life was the day my daughter was born. She was in such a hurry to get here; we barely made it to the hospital. I treasure so much about that day, and for all the love she's brought into my life from that moment on. I have her very first baby picture on my shelf in my den. I'll never take it down because it brings me back there, to that moment, every time I glance at it.

THE WRITER

What were you thinking on the day your kids were born?

Kelly

Chapter Eighteen

From: Aiden
Subject: The day my kids were born
To: Kelly

I was twenty-six when Ashley was born. We'd been married for a few years when we found out Michelle was pregnant. And even though we didn't plan it, it wasn't unwelcome.

Being in the military, it's just what you did. Family is what you had. When you left, you left them behind. You had them when you came home. So I guess it was just the natural order of things, if that makes sense.

I was busy, had just gotten a promotion. So the nine months went fast. Luckily, I was home when Ashley was born.

I was at work when Michelle called. Said she was on her way to the hospital, and I'd have to meet her there. I suppose I was the stereotypical husband/father from that point forward. I drove fast, got there and ran in. They pointed me in the right direction. Flew into the delivery room, where Michelle was almost ready to deliver. I was a mess.

But at the same time, it was beautiful.

I watched Ashley come into this world. This perfect, pink, screaming naked child who looked so vulnerable. I cried. I cut her cord. Watched as they did everything to her. Weighed her. Measured her.

Then they gave her to me. I held this impossibly small little girl and my world changed. She cooed, grabbed my finger as I counted hers. Michelle cried as she watched us. She said that was the most beautiful moment of her life. Seeing the two of us together.

I remember being so worried that Ashley would break. Or we'd get it wrong. Hurt her. It was such an unbelievably big responsibility, to get them home safe in the car. To keep her safe in the house. To make sure she had everything she needed to survive.

But you just do it, you know? It just happens, one day at a time.

Then Hannah came two and a half years later. And of course, we were more prepared. We were ready for her.

THE WRITER

I didn't think she'd surprise me, but she did.

Ashley was easy; Hannah wasn't. She fought to come in this world. They ended up doing a c-section, and that was a whole different experience. She didn't come out crying and flailing. She was blue. And they had to get her breathing.

And I cried again, this time because I was terrified. Yet still in awe of the whole thing.

I was so scared. And then she was there.

With just a little bit of work, she came to life. And once we heard that first tiny cry from her, everything changed. She let loose, and she let us know how big her personality was truly going to be. Big time. And she's never let us forget since.

Hannah's the one who shares her opinions. Her voice. Her frustrations. Her thoughts. Her desires. She'll never let you forget she's around. You always know where you stand with her. She takes center stage.

And even though she's always been the little sister, she knows exactly how to punch her big sister's buttons. They'd put on plays; Hannah was the dancer taking center stage while Ashley was the director standing back making sure she shined. They'd play on the playground and Hannah would jump off swings and fly off the monkey bars, doing a perfect flip, while Ashley stood by telling her how to make improvements.

Ashley's the thinker. Hannah's the doer.

Ashley's more like me. Hannah's more like her mom.

It's weird seeing yourself in your kids. But I see it all the time. Ashley questions if she can do something, then silently goes about it and gets it done. Yep, I do that all the time. I never ask for help, just do it. It's easier that way.

Then there's Hannah. The drama queen. Everything is a major production. She doesn't start with the end of the story; you have to hear every detail about how she got there.

Ashley would call from school and say "I got an A in the class, Dad."

Hannah calls and tells me about every person she worked with, every paper she wrote, the way the teacher dresses, how life was unfair because she didn't do quite as well as she expected. And only then would she tell me her grade. Usually an A as well.

They're good together. I'm glad they have each other.

It all goes so fast, doesn't it?

So now that you know all about my two little princesses, how about yours? What's the one trait Taylor has that you know she got from you?

Aiden

Chapter Nineteen

From: Kelly
Subject: My daughter has this...
To: Aiden

I started laughing when I read your question. A story jumped into my mind that we've teased each other about since she was a small child.

So let me set this up by explaining my wonderful, quirky trait of keeping neatness and order in my life.

I'm a balanced person; everything has to be equal, in balance. You might have noticed that in my home. I have a light on each side of the sofa, in the same spot on the end tables. Books are perfectly lined up on the shelf, sized from shortest to tallest. A frame on one side of the mantle, mirroring the one on the opposite side.

When Tom and I were first married, he decided to play with my "quirkiness." So he'd take things and move them out of order just to see what I'd do. I'd walk into a room and immediately have to adjust it to put it back in order. Makes sense, right?

After all, you can't have things out of balance. The world doesn't function that way.

It took me about three months to realize what he was doing. He just laughed, thought it was very amusing. He paid dearly for that. :)

Taylor was about three when I noticed one day that the books on her bookshelf were straightened and in order. I asked Tom if he had done it. Nope. So I messed them up. Sure enough, they went back to being in order. Smallest to largest. Everything in order. Colors all in a row.

So I started playing. I'd move things around, find out what bugged her. I didn't do it to annoy her; I just found it fascinating to see how much alike we were.

That doesn't make me a bad mom, does it!?

We've had a lot of laughs over that through the years.

Her "quirkiness" has held strong; you would see it if you went to her apartment today. I had to warn Jacob before they moved in together. Luckily he's similar. They do well together.

THE WRITER

Or maybe it's just young love!

Okay, I know you have one. The biggest "ohmigod" experience with your kids. The one that you think of instantly when you remember them growing up. The one that totally drove you crazy. Even now, you just wipe your hand over your face going, "Really?" I know you have one. What is it?

Kelly

Chapter Twenty

From: Aiden
Subject: My ohmigod experience
To: Kelly

Yep, you were right. Of course, I have one. In fact, I did just as you said, wiped my hand over my face as I thought about it. Right before I typed this. I still have nightmares.

It's called One Direction.

What is it with that band? What is it with girls and that band?

I was actually at home one day when Ashley came screaming into the house. Michelle wasn't there, but I was. She screamed that high pitch thing as she ran up to me, arms flailing, getting totally in my face. I thought somebody died.

"Can I Dad, huh, can I, can I?" Words all blended together, this screeching sound.

You know what I mean.

After I sat her down and made her start breathing again like a normal human being, Hannah comes in pretty much the same way.

I'm telling you I almost walked out of the house at that point.

Second girl, calm down, sit down. Deep breath.

Now, what is it?

Then they proceeded to tell me One Direction was coming to town, and they *had* to have tickets to go to the concert because everybody who was anybody would be going.

They gave me this huge, long story and before I knew it, I'd agreed to go, be a driver, the whole thing. I had no idea what I was getting myself into. And of course, Michelle just laughed her ass off at me when she found out. Made me follow through, wouldn't let me out of it.

And it began. That music, over and over again. Thank God for iPods. I don't know how our parents did it.

The car ride to the concert was miserable. Five screaming girls in my car with that Beautiful song over and over again.

That's what makes you beautiful. Ahhhhhhh!!!

THE WRITER

See, I even remember the words!

Every time it would end, one of them would yell AGAIN.

I had nightmares about that song for weeks!

Zayn! Harry! My girls became obsessed with them. I swear they talked about them like they were sitting at the kitchen table with us. Posters plastered all over their rooms.

Ugh.

I'm going on and on here. Obviously, this was my torture device for many, many weeks. Months actually.

The posters came down when they went to college. They still listen, I know they do. They even talk about them. Ashley was crushed when Zayn quit the band.

What does that say about me that I know Zayn quit the band?

Anyway, I will never admit this to anyone else. Please delete this and burn it after you read it. But I smile when I think back on that. Sort of. That's a part of them, their childhood.

And of course, I know that someday their kids will torture them just as bad. :)

That's truly what parenthood is all about. Counting the ways they'll face payback for the things they tortured you with. :)

So I know you said your daughter is happily living with her boyfriend. Are *you* happy your daughter is living with her boyfriend? We haven't reached that point yet, not quite sure how'd I feel if one of them made that move. How about you?

Aiden

Chapter Twenty-One

From: Kelly
Subject: When my daughter moved in with her boyfriend
To: Aiden

Is it wrong that I listened to One Direction while typing this?

LOL

I can honestly see your face wondering what the hell you signed up for. That's good for dads. Glad you did it!

I know I had mentioned before that Taylor was never really the dating type. I guess that's not saying much; I don't meet many kids these days that date at an early age. She "saw" a boy her senior year. But I think that was more about a group of friends hanging out, not really about dating. They never went out much, though they'd end up at parties together until they went off to college.

College was much the same way. Taylor decided to go to the University of Oregon instead of staying in California. That way she was close but not too close. Great school for her, she did well.

She did the dorm thing for a year. Moved into a house with a group of girls the second year. They kept that house through senior year, though the group changed a bit each fall. Senior year two guys moved in. Though they swore it was platonic, Nick did a lot with us that year. Dinners when we were there. He even came home with her for a long weekend. She said it was nothing, but ...

The whole thing died off after graduation, and I never heard much about him. But I knew he was her first true love. We talked about it a bit after we moved up here.

Then she got a job in Portland after graduation. That was three years ago. We were grateful - a job right away! You can't ask for more, right?

She loved it. Got her first place, a studio apartment in the middle of downtown, walking distance to work.

Then we moved up here. We started a Sunday thing where she could come over for Sunday dinner if she wanted to.

About six months before Tom died, she asked if she could bring a friend over. The friend turned out to be Jacob.

THE WRITER

Jacob is a year older than Taylor. They work together. He's in sales and travels quite a bit for conventions and food expos. She works in marketing. I think I mentioned it's a small company, so everyone pitches in wherever they're needed. So of course they started traveling together. And that turned into something more.

One Sunday turned into two. And before we knew it he was coming on all kinds of family outings. He traveled back to San Francisco for my mom's seventy-fifth birthday party. He did a weekend at the beach with us.

No matter how much you don't want to think of your kids growing up, in some ways, you do kind of daydream about who they will date, who they will marry. You start wishing for qualities and characteristics that you think are good. And yes, I'm sure a lot of it stems from what you see in the person you chose. So I'm sure I compared him somewhat to Tom.

But I have to say I couldn't have picked someone better myself. Jacob is just a really good guy. He comes from a great family. He has a great head on his shoulders.

Yep, I like him a lot.

Then Tom.

Of course, I didn't watch their relationship much during that time. I was just trying to survive.

But looking back, he was a rock. He was there for her, all the time. He didn't ask, he just did. They'd come over on Sundays and make me eat. Often, it was Jacob that cooked.

Again, this is all in retrospect, but something changed during that period. About six months ago they moved in together. And they've been steadfast ever since.

They complete each other. They're good for each other.

They put out this vibration like everything works when they're together.

I know nobody likes thinking about their kids growing up and having lives. But it happens. And honestly, I'm so happy that she found someone who cares for her as much as he does. I think that's the most important thing of all.

They're not talking marriage or anything. What millennial does? Not that I'd want them to do the whole wedding production if they like what they have already. I'm a happy mama either way.

But they're committed. They're happy. And I like to think my relationship with Tom influenced that.

So, a fairytale ending? I guess we'll wait and see. But for now their "happy ever after" is going strong.

Okay, speaking of fairytales, let's talk books. I'm a writer, so my conversations always turn to books.

THE WRITER

What's your favorite book?

Kelly

Chapter Twenty-Two

From: Aiden
Subject: Favorite Book
To: Kelly

The moment I read your question, I thought back to the conversation we had out on your balcony. I haven't read in such a long time, never really had the time.

Working on a ship doesn't give you much time for stuff like that. Then when I was home, it was all about being there for everyone else. The kids took up all of my time when I was with them. I devoted my time to them, knowing eventually I'd have to go months without seeing them again.

So I never picked up a book, not because I don't like to read, but because I fell asleep if I did.

I never really thought much about the production side of them either until you told me about what you do for a living. Suddenly I was curious.

So I decided to put my Kindle app to use. Before we left, I downloaded all of your books. But I gravitated to *Finding Love Again* first. I finished it in two days out at sea. Then I read your other books. I think I had them all read in less than two weeks. But something made me keep returning to *Finding Love Again*. Yes, I'll admit it, I've read it a half dozen times.

Somehow it's made me feel closer to you. Opened up your world to me, showed me how you think.

I know, it's a novel. It's fiction. But even after spending just a few hours with you and getting to know you here through email, I see so much of you in that book.

I know you used your writing to work through issues. Because in many cases, I had similar issues.

Like when Serena was yelling at Chloe:

"I'm tired of this shit. I want to feel whole again. I want to feel like me again. I want to wake up and not have this overwhelming despair sit on my chest. I want to be done with this pain. I want to wake up and hear the birds sing. See the sunshine and savor it as it beats down on my face. I want to feel sexy when I walk out the door. I want to feel horny when I see a good looking guy. I want normal. I just want more. And I know I'll get there. Because I'm not willing to live in this dark world forever. I don't want to, and I don't think he would want me to either. I

THE WRITER

want to feel. I want to breathe. I want life. I crave it. And I'll get there, I really will. Patience, okay? I'm getting there. Don't push. I know I want it all and know I'll get there eventually. And I love you for kicking me in the ass, I really do. I need you to do that, as a matter of fact. But don't get mad when I push back. Because every step forward means a step away from all that I once loved. And as much as I know that's what I need, I want to rock back into it sometimes and feel all the wonder and amazement that was him."

I love those words. I think I've read that section a hundred times. Yep, have it highlighted, so it's easy to get to.

It puts into words all that I've felt.

I'm not a talker. A) Not my personality. B) I'm a guy. :)

Though it can be argued that I'm a much better typer and communicator now, thanks to you and these emails. I don't think I've ever "talked" so much in my life.

I haven't read a book in ages. And now I've read several, all yours, all about your world, the way you think, the way you process.

What a magical gift you give others, I can see now that's what writers really do. They allow you to escape your own world and move into something else. They allow you to feel things you might not have worked out in your own mind up until that point. They give you new perspectives. And in the case of *Finding Love Again*, hope.

Hope that eventually, all this shit that has happened will eventually not hurt so bad. And it will subside enough to let the good start happening once again.

I want to feel all those things. Alive. Happy.

I want to feel like a guy. A normal guy that doesn't have the world pressing down on his shoulders, covered in so much muck he doesn't know how to come up for air.

I'm breathing. I'm feeling. I'm getting there.

You know, I think *Finding Love Again* would make an excellent movie. One of those chick flicks my wife always made me go to when we had a Saturday night to ourselves. Secretly, I always enjoyed them because they made her smile. And I've discovered I really enjoy making the people in my life smile.

So that's my question back to you. What's your favorite movie? What movie puts a smile on your face?

Aiden

Chapter Twenty-Three

From: Kelly
Subject: Favorite movie
To: Aiden

OMG, you're going to make me pick just one?

Impossible.

Yep, I'm the chick flick queen. Naturally, right? I mean, where do you think my inspiration comes from?

Oh yeah, living. ;)

But living also means reading every gushy romance novel I can get my hands on. And watching every mushy chick flick I can find.

The Notebook. I mean, hello? It's The Notebook. How can you watch that movie and not get wrapped up in all the emotion and romance of the whole thing? Now that's true love.

The Holiday. We have about a half dozen movies that we pull out every Christmas that we have to watch. Christmas Vacation. The Christmas Story. Those are great family movies. But I have to see The Holiday; it's my favorite. Jude Law is just so damn sexy in that movie. His good guy attitude gets me every time. Truly *The Holiday* we all want to have, right? Okay, maybe it's just me …

Dirty Dancing. Is there a more classic movie than this? Patrick Swayze has got to be one of the most lovable leading romantic men ever. I think it's his whole story. He always seemed like one of the nicest guys on the planet. Dying young only made that image stronger.

Pretty Woman. Richard Gere. Need I say more? Then there's the entire princess fantasy around it. Totally unrealistic. But still. The shopping scene? Being jetted away for the perfect date in an airplane? Getting the guy of your dreams? It doesn't get any better than that.

Before Midnight. I know this wasn't as commercialized as the others I mentioned, but I loved this movie. It was a beautiful look at relationships in the rawest form. Thick with emotion, it's all about two people, their lives together, how they met, how they fell in love, and whether it all was worth it for the chance at love and happiness. It's the last of a trilogy featuring the same two people in each film, created over eighteen years of time. I watch them again and again just for the cleverness between these two people.

As you can tell, I have a problem picking a favorite when it comes to any form of entertainment, books or movies.

So maybe I'll say I love a movie that makes me happy, makes me think.

I'm not much on blood and gore just for the sake of it. If it has a purpose, if it's part of the story, sure.

I love great stories. I love seeing them on the big screen. I love getting completely and emotionally involved, figuring out exactly what the writers are trying to express.

I love finding the hidden meanings. If a story has a moral, I love seeing how they incorporate it into the scenes.

I love relationships. I love watching how other people handle all kinds of situations. What makes people laugh. What makes them cry. What gets them pissed off beyond belief. What gets them excited. What is unforgivable. What draws people together. What causes them to fall apart.

Fascinating.

I guess that's my English/writer/psychology traits shining through.

I love ending a day watching a great movie. Then talking about it late into the evening, diving into the characters, figuring out how human nature is so much the same. Even though we try to make it so complicated, we're all pretty much the same.

Obviously reading and watching great movies is a big part of my life. I can't imagine a day going by without both of them being a part of it. If you were to describe your perfect day, what would it look like? What would you do? Where would you be?

Kelly

Chapter Twenty-Four

From: Aiden
Subject: My perfect day
To: Kelly

Maybe we'll have to kick back and watch movies sometime. I haven't seen all of the ones you mentioned.

Of course, you might have to throw in an action flick here and there to keep me happy. :)

My perfect day.

Only three requirements. No place to be. About seventy-five degrees. A beach.

From there, other things can be added in along the way.

A beach with white sand, very few people, and a great view are always nice.

I love it just warm enough to walk in the water barefoot without freezing.

A table set up on the beach with the best food ever.

Great conversation. Talking about everything and nothing all at the same time.

A hammock. A beach chair. I'm not particular. But a nap in the sunshine sounds heavenly.

This is really difficult. It's one of the toughest emails I've written.

Because when I say "my perfect day," my mind naturally goes back to some of the best days from my past. Things I've always enjoyed. My happiest memories.

So, of course, they go to vacations I've taken in the past.

But you worded it differently. What would your perfect day look like? What would I do? That sounds like my future. If I could plan it today, what would it include?

That's meshing my past with my present and future, and that's where I get stuck.

I know what I love. What feels incredible.

THE WRITER

But after losing a part of me, how do I get back there? How do I find my way back and feel that again?

That part came alive again, just a little bit, when I spent time with you.

So in some ways, I'm sitting here merging what I love from my past and combining it with what I'd love to share with you.

Is that weird? Creepy?

I don't want to go too fast. But I don't know how else to do this.

I think about you. I wonder where this will lead. I dream …

I'm fifty. Life is short. So I guess I'll throw caution to the wind.

This is it. This is me. I can see you in the perfect day I'd plan for myself soon.

Next question: You've mentioned your bucket list a few times. What's your biggest bucket list item you've never shared with anyone? That crazy-ass thing you've never told anyone about, but secretly you're dying to do?

Aiden

Chapter Twenty-Five

From: Kelly
Subject: Bucket list item
To: Aiden

I get it. I *so* get it.

How do you move forward when your past wasn't bad? In fact, it was pretty fantastic.

This has been so hard because I didn't fall out of love. I had things great. Until ...

And yet we have no choice, do we? We have to move forward, just because.

My brother asked me when I first told him about you if it was grief that brought us together as quickly as it did. And I've thought about that a lot. We have such similar backgrounds in so many ways. Was it the similarity of our situation that seduced us?

No. Not at all. It was you. It was how I clicked with you. That energy that attracted me to you from the moment you sat next to me. I feel it in these emails, the way you write.

Your thoughts. Your dreams. How you reason. The way you talk about the people you love. Your stories.

I feel it too.

And after fifty-three years on earth, I know I'm ready for a little of the good stuff again too. I'm not afraid of the bad, I've lived through so much. And I can honestly say that I see life on the other side.

I want to know you better. I want to learn more about you. I would love to be a part of your perfect day.

So, you want to know something from my bucket list.

In case you couldn't tell, I'm a very in-control person. :) Everything has its place on my to-do list. I have goal lists a mile long. Even my bucket list is built around my organized lifestyle. So I've had things like "sell 10,000 books in one day" on it. Yep, boring, right?

Everything is controlled, calculated, figured, placed into a bigger picture. Things don't go onto my bucket list unless I've had time to think about it for a while.

THE WRITER

Beth and I were talking about my bucket list the night I met you. As she so wisely put it, my bucket list was filled with things Tom and I planned out together. As we stood there, she looked at all the Navy guys around us and dared me to have a one night stand to get back in the saddle again. Totally out of character. I told her she was crazy.

But what she said hasn't been lost on me. My bucket list was all about "we" instead of "me" and I have been attempting to update it lately. My goal is to live a little more out of my comfort zone. To do things that stretch me, allow me to do things I've never done before.

So I added something to it a couple of weeks ago. It reads like this:

> *Do something totally crazy, something totally spontaneous that is so beyond what I normally would do it'll leave people who know me best saying, "WHAT?"*

I know it's not specific. Not a normal bucket list item. But it has meaning to me. I don't know what that'll be yet. I've got time.

And I'll know when it's right. It'll stretch me beyond anything I've done before. It'll leave me feeling a bit out of control to say "yes" to it.

I mean, I've lived through the most out-of-control times of my life. And I still have no idea where I'm going to land. I'm working on that every day.

So to say yes to something spontaneously with little planning, little thought, just do it? How fun would that be? Not a little thing, but a great big, life-changing thing.

Who knows, it'll happen. One of these days ...

We've shared so much. I feel like a lot has changed between us. I know we keep flipping back and forth, talking about our pasts, reaching for the future. You can't have one without the other; I get that. That's what makes us who we are. So I have a difficult question for you. We've both admitted we've come back from the bottom, climbed slowly out from the worst place possible. It's something I think we've both come to terms with in our own ways. What was your worst day and how did it change you?

Kelly

Chapter Twenty-Six

From: Aiden
Subject: The worst day of my life
To: Kelly

When you asked this question, I bet you thought you could guess the worst day of my life. The day my wife died, right?

In some ways, that day was a truly horrible day. But it wasn't the worst. Not by a long shot.

Because everybody was here. My two girls. My parents. My brother. Michelle's mom. Her sister. Mike and Janet. They were all here, surrounding us. Loving us. Supporting us.

When it happened, there were lots of things to do. Things to prepare for. It kept me busy. I didn't think.

Sure, I cried. But I existed. I moved because I had to. I had to keep going because there were plans to make and things to do.

I had to make sure my girls were okay. I had to think about my parents. Make sure Michelle's mom was safe. Michelle's death just drained her, and we were all worried she was going to collapse.

Then the funeral. Hard. But I moved from one person to the next, faking my way through talking with everyone, hearing how sorry they were, pretending like I had it together.

I'm fine. They became my favorite words for way too long.

The funny thing is life eventually moves on.

My daughters went back to school. My parents went back to Maryland. People went back to work. Life went on.

That's when I realized I was alone.

I eventually had to go back to work. I made the choice to get back on this ship.

So I was busy putting everything together. Packing and getting ready to leave. That's when I realized Michelle wouldn't be at home to keep everything running while I was gone. She was always here. I just walked away, and she kept everything running. She kept everything working. I'd just let her do her job while I did mine. We never thought about it; we just did it because that was our lives together.

THE WRITER

Until it wasn't. It wasn't about packing anymore. I had to close up the house because nobody was going to be there until I got back. It would sit empty for months.

I collapsed. Mike found me later, on the floor. He sat me up, let me cry. I don't even remember much. Just caved into everything.

Eventually, he got me up, shoved me in the shower, sat with me all day and all night. He pulled me through. Janet promised to take care of my home. Mike made sure I was on that ship when it sailed.

He's supported me every day since.

Collapsing was the worst day of my life. I don't want to ever do that again.

Your turn.

When did you know you were okay?

Aiden

Chapter Twenty-Seven

From: Kelly
Subject: I'm okay ... really
To: Aiden

I so get everything you're saying. A little different because Tom left in the morning and never came home again. I went through shock and horror and everything in between in the course of a few hours. I seriously wanted to die.

But of course the moment everyone heard the news, they flocked here and surrounded me for weeks. I don't think I was alone for a moment for the first month. Like you, eventually, I was at home and realized something needed to be done that Tom had always done. I crumbled because I suddenly realized I had to do it. Me. Not us. Not him. Me.

Sucked big time.

But eventually I had to do it, and I did it. I didn't like it very much, but I started developing my own routine. I got things done. My way.

And I muddled through the first year, doing all the little things that had to be done. I had successes with my writing. I made some new friends. Traveled a bit on my own. (Okay, to my Mom and Dad's in San Diego where I spent two weeks writing. But hey, I got on the plane! I was making headway!)

Then a few months ago Beth started hounding me about getting out, making new friends. In her case, friends = dating.

I've had a few choice words with her along the way as she tries to weave her magic into my love-life.

And she has set me up with a couple of doozies. A fifty-year-old that had more medical conditions than most eighty-year-olds. And another that literally felt me up in the restaurant!

But I could never be mad at her for long. I wouldn't be here without Beth and Chris. I'm not kidding when I say they are the reason I survived.

So I put up with her little quirks and misguided matchmaking! I roll my eyes, get through it, and move on.

You did see me rolling my eyes at her when she came over and asked if you wanted to sit with us, right?

Here we go again, I thought to myself. But, that's Beth.

THE WRITER

I sat down next to you and had this tingle pass through me when I looked at you. And I thought, hmmm. Interesting. I haven't remotely felt anything like that in a very long time.

Then we chatted about Maryland. And the coincidence was ... interesting.

We laughed. We clicked. I don't know; things just seemed to roll between us.

And it continued from there, very quickly.

When we both confessed our losses, something washed over me. A feeling I've never had before.

A feeling that said someone else out there felt what I felt, moved on too because he had no choice.

Not because you wanted to or even chose to. But because you had to.

You know the pain. You've lived it.

You get the fact that every day you take one more step because you have to.

Then Saturday, I found myself counting down the minutes until you showed up. And Sunday. Wondering what you were doing. And Monday, thinking about you heading out to sea, calling my brother and telling him all about you.

I sat down for lunch after talking with Chris on Monday, and I was overwhelmed to discover I hadn't thought about Tom all weekend. Not really. I mean we talked about him. But not the true "think" about him like I've done every day since.

It was you instead. I thought about you. Wondering what you were doing.

I thought about the future instead of the past. I thought about seeing you. Wondering what it would be like this fall to spend more than a couple of nights with you.

I was excited about doing something totally brand new. Not something I'd done in the past, in some other life, in some other way. I wanted a new memory. I wanted something different. I wanted to create something new. With you.

And I didn't feel guilty about it. Not really.

I smiled. I imagined my life. Because I'm living. And I want to live. I choose to live.

I want to have fun. I want new experiences.

So I finally had to admit, I'm going to be okay.

Wow. What a rush!

Eighteen months, that's not bad, right? Not saying I'm anywhere near okay. It's a lifetime process. But still. Here I am, ready to try again. Pretty cool.

THE WRITER

Don't want to scare you because I talk about you. Thinking about you. Spending time with you. Obviously, we're getting to know each other here. And I'm just enjoying. I'm not latching on like some crazy woman or anything. (Just thought I should say, er, type that. But then you kinda said it too.)

But it really took you for me to realize that I'm ready to move forward. I owe you a lot for that. So thank you!

As long as we're 'fessing up here, what do you miss most about being married?

Kelly

Chapter Twenty-Eight

From: Aiden
Subject: Miss about being married
To: Kelly

I've read your last email a hundred times, processing. Because in so many ways, I could have written it too.

It's the coincidences that shook my world too. Maryland. Our spouses. The way we joked. The way we laughed.

I have to tell you; something hit me when I walked through the door of your condo that night. The view. The music you had playing. This big "wow" passed through me. I didn't process it at the time. I just remember feeling that as I walked in.

And when I met you in the kitchen, it felt familiar. Comfortable. Like it was a place I was supposed to be. We fell into a routine, talking, cooking, sharing. That tiny act of being together in a totally intimate way without touching or being all over each other. Just being content, relaxed while doing the normal things that need to be done.

Remember when you were first married, you couldn't get enough of each other? If you were in the same room, you were all over each other? But as time went on, it was that underlying feeling of being loved, being understood that made every moment worthwhile.

I loved being in the kitchen, making dinner with Michelle. We'd brush by each other as we chopped or stirred. We'd bump into each other as the kids ran in and out of the room. We'd laugh at something stupid because it brought back a memory that only we had together. We understood because it came together for us.

We had a wicked sense of humor together. We laughed together all the time.

The rule to a good marriage, or so everybody says, is not to go to bed angry. We always said it was having at least one good laugh a day. Sometimes it wasn't about falling down laughing. It was the humor that creeps into your eyes because you share a joke that only you two know.

Or getting the giggles as you're lying in bed together.

Or laughing just because it's all so damn good, and you just want it to go on and on, forever.

THE WRITER

God, I want to laugh again. A full-fledged belly laugh where tears spring from my eyes and I can't get them under control.

And right now, I'm imagining laughing like that with you.

Have you ever been to Vietnam before?

Aiden

Chapter Twenty-Nine

From: Kelly
Subject: Vietnam
To: Aiden

Kind of a "yes or no" question, isn't it? So my answer is:

No. Never been there. Nowhere close.

Kelly

Chapter Thirty

From: Aiden
Subject: Meet Me
To: Kelly

Meet me in Ho Chi Minh City, Vietnam the first week of August.

Aiden

CHAPTER THIRTY-ONE

From: Kelly
Subject: re: Meet Me
To: Aiden

Yes!

Kelly

Chapter Thirty-Two

From: Aiden
Subject: Counting down the days
To: Kelly

I don't even know what to type. I'm so excited.

This is crazy, right?

So here are the details. I booked everything on my end, so I'm set to go.

I have leave from the first to the tenth.

I arrive at Ho Chi Minh City's Tan Son Nhat International Airport at 11:30 am on the first, leave on the tenth at 1:40 pm.

I'll take care of everything, hotel, car, all the details. So all you have to do is get yourself there around those times and we'll go from there.

Any special requests? Anything you want to do?

Aiden

Chapter Thirty-Three

From: Kelly
Subject: Counting down the days too
To: Aiden

I have a very special request. To see you!

That's it. Otherwise I'm not fussy.

Crazy, I booked a flight for under eight hundred. I figured it would be outrageous with only three weeks to go. Guess I'm going to have to fly more ... care to join me? (We may have to talk about that while we're together. Together. Very strange in a very good way!)

So here are my flight details. I mirrored your flights as much as I could, United flight 2360 arrives 4:30 pm on the first, leave at 12:40 pm on the tenth.

I'll see you in three weeks.

And I just checked off the crazy, spontaneous thing off my bucket list!

My next question: Have *you* been to Vietnam before?

Kelly

Chapter Thirty-Four

From: Aiden
Subject: Visiting Vietnam
To: Kelly

Yes, I've been there several times. Comes with the territory since we're always floating around in this part of the world. It's a beautiful city, I've always enjoyed being there. Though up until this point, it's always been long weekends and one or two of the guys. We always talked about turning it into a family vacation at some point, just never did it. I think I'm changing my ways here. I want to do a lot more of this kind of stuff too. I've never made quick decisions like this before, doing something just because.

I am so looking forward to this. You have no idea.

To see you.

To touch you.

So now that we have the details all planned out, I have a big question for you I've been contemplating since I read your book for the first time. I wasn't quite sure how to ask/email, but now I'm just going to do it.

How on earth do you write the love scenes the way you do?

Maybe I've read them a few times. And maybe I've thought about you when I do. :)

But, wow. Let's just say I had NO idea romance novels were like that.

Aiden

Chapter Thirty-Five

From: Kelly
Subject: Those WOW scenes
To: Aiden

LOL. I've laughed about your question quite a bit (in a good way) imagining you reading some of those scenes for the first time. Never knew what your wife/mother/daughters were reading before, did you? Okay, that was probably too much for you to think about. :)

Where to begin.

I've been in marketing forever. Always loved writing and creating. I've kept a journal since I was a little girl. So writing has always been a part of my life.

Reading too. I was the child that huddled beneath the blankets with a flashlight at night, so that I could get in one more chapter. Drove my dad crazy. He'd find me like that at midnight sometimes if it were a particularly good book.

So I've read everything. Love mysteries. Read my fair share of non-fiction and literary work. And of course, a good romance on the beach never hurts.

Not much difference between romance novels and chick flicks. They're all designed to make you feel good. Okay, that can be taken a lot of ways, and I'll just leave it at that.

I attended a fiction writer's workshop about seven years ago just for fun. But I kind of fell in love with it. I started writing down ideas, playing with short stories. Added the "write an epic novel" to my bucket list.

When Tom took the new job, with his salary and stock options and our investments, I didn't have to go back to work. So I used that as my excuse to become a writer.

I had several short stories I started working from. None were really romance based, just more life-based, I guess. I never thought about romance before. But I'm not the kind of person that wanted to write a book and never have it read. I wanted fans. I wanted a business. So I started looking at where the biggest successes were. And that, of course, kept leading me to romance.

I picked up a few mentors and read everything I could. I took a few online courses, joined the Romance Writers Association and

THE WRITER

learned even more. Yep, I'm all in or nothing, so I did everything.

So all of that is the long way of saying I had absolutely ZERO experience writing love scenes when I headed down this path.

Life experience? Yes. Writing experience? Nope.

I read everything I could get my hands on about writing a love scene. I read dozens of books trying to get the feel for how writers knocked out those scenes. I'd read other romance books. I'd highlight scenes I liked for inspiration.

Then I wrote. First book, first scene ... sucked.

I went back, and I thought about the characters. Who they were. What they would be feeling. How they would react. What they would do in that situation. And I wrote again.

I put on sexy music. I create playlists with romantic love songs and use them to make me feel the moment as I write.

I read other work. I watch movies. And I take notes. Yes, weird. But if they touch on a topic in a way that I think is particularly interesting, it may spawn an idea that I can use. So I write those down and use them when I get stuck in my writing.

Then I write over and over again. I read it out loud. Does it seem realistic? Would things actually happen that way?

Eventually, I say yes.

Oh, and I guess my editor agrees. When we both feel the editing is complete, the moment is complete.

Difficult? Yes. Time consuming? Yes.

It's all about human emotions. You have to take notice of how a person feels, thinks and reacts every moment of the situation. Then put that in writing to tell the story.

Not that romantic. A lot of work. But it's fun!

So there you have it. The not-so-glamourous life of a romance writer!

Okay, I sense our Q&A sessions are changing direction here a bit.

So I've been I've been thinking about something since I said yes to Vietnam. Are you as nervous as I am about seeing each other again? I just keep reliving those few hours we had together. I know so much more about you now, it's amplified my feelings for you. But still, seeing you again face to face. I gotta say I'm nervous. You too?

Kelly

Chapter Thirty-Six

From: Aiden
Subject: My nerves
To: Kelly

That completely blew my mind about writing. Thanks for sharing. I never really thought how difficult that would be to get the feelings correct with just a few words.

I guess it must be the same for movies, never thought about that before either. Making sure you portray something that is very personal in such an intimate way. Must be hard for actors, especially when they don't have an intimate connection already built in. They had some action flick on last night, and I sat through a love scene, made me appreciate the art form of it in a new way.

Yes, it's not just you. I'm nervous. I'm anxious. I'm excited. I'm also exhilarated. Alive.

You are definitely all I've been thinking of for weeks now. Insane, isn't it? To think we met only by some of the most crazy-ass circumstances imaginable. And now? This is what I look forward to more than anything. Your emails mean the world to me, help me make it through my days.

They're also giving me inspiration for what I want to do next. And trust me, I've been thinking a lot about that lately. That's part of where Vietnam came from. I'm ready to live again. It's time.

You remember when Lieutenant Stevenson dropped you off on deck, and you were waiting for me?

I walked up the stairs and saw you standing there, watching one of the tour groups go by. You literally took my breath away.

Maybe it's age. Maybe it's experience. I haven't dated much (at all) since Michelle, but I've never felt even a spark with anyone until you. I swear it was like walking into an electrical storm.

When I stood beside you, the backs of our hands were touching, I felt like I was on fire.

I still see you, feel that when I think of you.

And I can't wait to experience that again. Because I know it's still there, I can feel it when I open up every email you send.

THE WRITER

Nervous? Yes, in a very good way.

I'm counting down the days.

My turn. I'm going to let you interpret this any way you choose. Where's your spot?

Aiden

Chapter Thirty-Seven

From: Kelly
Subject: My spot
To: Aiden

You are sooo wrong.

You told me in your first email you weren't a very good writer.

WRONG.

I had to take a cold shower after that last email. Or put Magic Mike to good use.

I'll let you interpret that any way you choose ...

Sooo ...

LORI OSTERBERG

My spot.

You know when you kiss right behind the ear ...

And you move down ...

The back of the neck ...

Down ...

That sweet spot by the collarbone ...

I go weak at the knees if I'm not holding on ...

Kelly

Chapter Thirty-Eight

From: Kelly
Subject: Another shower
To: Aiden

Sooo ... did I make you take a shower too?

Man, we've moved to a whole new playing field, haven't we?

Didn't want to ruin the mood with the last email. ;)

So here's my question.

What are your expectations? I'm assuming it's you and me, all day, all night, every moment with you. Learning who we are. You good with that assumption?

I'm clean, nobody since Tom. And "technically" I can still get pregnant, so if you haven't had a vasectomy, we need to plan.

I can't wait to touch you again. And spend the entire night with you. That's my one regret from that weekend. I wish we would have had more time to explore each other. I've relived those two nights so many times. When we were in the gardens, I remember watching you laugh, wondering how I could feel like I'd known you for so long when we'd only just met the night before.

That physical connection is something that still amazes me every day. I guess that's why I like writing about it because it's so rare. There are so few people on earth that I've ever felt it with. I felt it with Tom. I've felt it with a couple of my friends. Beth. Kari, my BFF from college.

And you.

What are the chances the two of us arrived at that one place in time, shoulder to shoulder at a table at Henry's?

One in a million.

I'm counting down the days …

Kelly

Chapter Thirty-Nine

From: Aiden
Subject: Us
To: Kelly

I honestly have never done this before. Emailing this way, I mean.

I'm clean. Nobody since Michelle. Vasectomy.

It was tough leaving you that night. As we made our way back down the river, out to sea, I sat there staring off into the darkness wondering what the hell I was doing. How something could happen this fast.

We're both in the same boat, married "forever." Can't say I've done anything like this in a very long time. And here I was, finding something when I wasn't even looking.

I sat there questioning everything. Should I email you? Was it all for real? Should it just be a really great one night stand?

Yet I knew I wanted more. I knew I wanted to discover who you were. So with a lot of courage, I emailed you that first time with not a clue as to what to say.

This question/answer thing was a great idea. I know this is probably one of the strangest dating rituals ever. But it's worked.

And when you said yes to Vietnam, that one word changed my world.

I'm retiring. I've been thinking about it for several years. I quit thinking about it once Michelle was diagnosed, stayed after because I had no idea what else to do.

Now I no longer care what I do. I just don't want to do this anymore. So I'm not. I put in my paperwork today. Done deal in December. When I get back in September, I'll never have to do this again.

I don't know where this will lead. And all I want to do for these ten days we have together is spend them with you, see where it takes us. Nothing more.

Just wanted you to know.

Aiden

Chapter Forty

From: Kelly
Subject: Retiring
To: Aiden

Wow. You have been doing some thinking. Big step.

I can tell you're ready.

In some ways I guess that's what I did when we moved here to Portland. No more nine to five. No job commitments. No working for someone else.

I can't imagine not doing this now.

It started out as something I wanted in my life. Then it became my therapy in so many ways. Now it's just a kick-ass time. I feel so lucky being able to do what I do.

And here's the beauty of it. I can do this from anywhere. Have laptop, will travel.

I've met so many people that are doing just that. They aren't tied down to a house; they move whenever the mood strikes them. They don't call any one place home.

I met one woman at a writing retreat in Arizona earlier this year. She calls herself a sun chaser. She moves every four months to someplace new in the world, looks for a place that will have four months of beautiful weather. Then finds a great airbnb and lives there. If she likes it, she may go back the next year. If not, there are a gazillion other places to land. The beaches motivate her. Sunshine lets her go whenever she desires.

Great, yes?

I've been going over a lot of the same things in my mind.

As Beth keeps reminding me, my life before was always about "us." My bucket list - "us." I went from college to Tom. And therefore everything we did, everything we ever planned for had "two" involved instead of one. It's been a big transition for me to realize it's now about me, what I want and where I want to go.

Part of that has terrified me for months.

Yet I really wouldn't change anything right now. I love what I do. My daughter's close. My family is close; I can fly in to visit

THE WRITER

in less than a couple of hours. Travel? It's coming ... Vietnam, baby!

So I guess looking at me right now, I have to say I've finally reached some level of happiness again. I'm taking it all one day at a time. I'm where I want to be. I'm doing what I want to do.

And that includes you.

I agree. Ten days in Vietnam. And we'll see where it goes from there.

Kelly

Chapter Forty-One

Kelly snickered as she looked at her phone. Twelve minutes. "Hi."

She wandered out onto her patio, settled in for a long conversation.

"So I hear you're traveling to Vietnam." Chris kept his voice light.

She could hear the hint of concern in his voice. "I take it you've talked with your wife."

"You can't tell her something like that and not expect it to get back to me immediately."

"I know. I figured it'd give you two a chance to talk about me before you called and tried to talk me out of it."

"What makes you think I'd talk you out of it?"

Kelly laughed. "Really? I've only known you for fifty-three years. I can hear your conversation with Lisa. *She's what?*"

Chris took a deep breath, knowing full well he'd been caught in the act. "Well, what did you expect? You think it's wise to travel all the way to Vietnam for someone you barely know?"

That set off a storm in her. "Really? You want to go there? We've talked about this. You have no idea what Aiden means to me or how important he's become. I may just say 'we're emailing' but it's turned into a whole lot more."

The pause went on forever. She could hear Chris take a small breath, hear him putting his thoughts together, yet unsure of what to say.

Let him stew. Well, at least for a bit.

Kelly valued his opinion. But dammit, she was allowed to live her life any way she chose. And if that meant checking off 'spontaneous adventure' from her bucket list by traveling to Vietnam to see Aiden again, that was her prerogative.

Chris dove in carefully. "What do you mean more? All you've said is email. What's going on?"

Kelly took a breath to suppress the annoyance she knew he'd hear. "Stop already. We're emailing. Daily. Sometimes twice or three times a day. We've covered a lot of ground. I know a lot about Aiden. I know enough about him to know that I want more. And that means visiting him in Vietnam to see what this truly is."

"That's what worries me."

"What? Me seeing someone worries you? Why?"

"Are you ready for all this? Not even two years yet. You haven't even dated. And now you're dropping everything and going halfway around the world for a guy?"

"Ohmigod, I'm not going to *marry* him. I've been through hell. He's been through hell. We're both getting back into this thing called life. I'm fifty-three, he's fifty. We're two intelligent people who might have an interest in each other. That's it. And

THE WRITER

it's not up to you where we go from here. That's between Aiden and me. Us. Nobody else. That includes you, big brother."

She heard him huff out a breath. Then with a catch in his voice say, "I know. I just don't want to see you get hurt."

Which of course broke her heart just a little bit. He'd been there right beside her from the moment it happened. She knew he'd protect her from everything if it were possible. That's what she loved most about him. He was her big brother, and nothing would ever change their relationship.

"I've been hurt. Massively. And I'm coming back." Kelly moved a hand across her forehead, tucked her hair behind her ear. "Chris, I know this is hard. It's been a long, hard road from the day of the accident. But you've always told me to move forward, just a little bit, one day at a time. That's what I'm doing. This is what I want to do." She heard him quietly sniff, knew she'd touched a nerve. He'd always hid his emotions to protect her. To be there for her, supporting her. "I love you. I know you've been through a lot too. I appreciate you more than you will ever know."

Kelly said those words often, knew she'd say them often, for the rest of their lives. "Maybe this is my shot at a little bit of happiness for a change. Trust me; it's better than the alternative."

"I know," Chris said quietly.

"If I could bring Tom back, right now, right here, I'd do it. I'd give up anything, my house, my car, my clothes, my career. I'd give away everything for Tom to be right beside me once again. Because when we moved to Portland, it was like a light came on again. We lit up together. We were doing the empty nest thing perfectly. It was like when we were in college. We fell in love all over again. We were having fun."

She gulped to keep a sob at bay. "We were good together. I loved him more than anything. I thought about him all the time. I texted him things you don't even want to know. We were truly having our second love affair."

Kelly closed her eyes, seeing Tom in her mind. She laid her head back against the chair. "I want him. I would do anything to have him back."

She shook her head, sat up straight.

"But here's the thing. It doesn't work that way. I don't get a do-over. He's gone. And I can't change that. I have to accept that. I have, I do, as much as I don't want to. I miss him so much sometimes; you have no idea. You can say you sympathize, but you truly have no idea. You can't understand the pain I feel laying there in bed sometimes, not even being able to get up because I'm doubled over from grief. I can't even cry, just sob. Try and catch my breath because it hurts so damn bad I feel like I'm dying.

"After weeks, months of going through this, I've learned that life is short. And I want to enjoy. I want to have fun. I want to live."

She rested her elbows on her knees. "Chris, I know this is hard. But I have good days now. And I don't know if I have two years or fifty years left of my life. But I don't want to live closed up in a shell because I lost my one true love. He's a part of me, always will be. That's not going to change. But what if I can have a little fun? What if I can have something else, with someone else too? Why not?

"This isn't about Tom; this is about me. Because Tom ended when I was fifty-one. He doesn't know the fifty-three-year-old me I've become. He won't influence the sixty-year-old me, not from day-to-day living anyway. That's all me now. And who I

THE WRITER

choose to introduce into my life from this point forward is my decision."

Chris softened his voice. "I get that baby, I really do. I guess I'm just playing the big brother here. I know how hard it's been. I've watched you suffer. I'd do anything to keep that away from you. And part of me is still recovering, too. Tom was one of my closest friends. I thought the four of us would travel together in retirement. I never imagined it would be anything but the four of us. I knew you'd do this eventually, I guess I always thought you'd start small. You know, see someone there in Portland." She could hear the hint of a smile in his voice. "But traveling to the other side of the planet? Wow, that's something."

"I know, but it's kind of exciting too, right?" She giggled, just a little, and heard him snicker in response. "I have no idea if Aiden is right for me or how long we'll last. All I know is those two nights he was here; I had a little bit of magic return to my life. I played. I had fun. I laughed. I relaxed. Aiden got me. We fit. We clicked. And dammit, Chris, I know you know what that's like, even if you and Lisa have been together for eons. You don't click with most people. And when you do, it's good. I want more. I felt it with him beside me. I feel it in the way we write each other. I felt it in the goosebumps I got when I said yes to Vietnam." She took a big breath and let it out slowly.

"And I'm going." She waited for his response.

"Vietnam, huh?"

"I know, right?"

"So where? When? And why Vietnam?"

"I'm meeting him in Ho Chi Minh City, the first ten days of August. He took leave, guess that's close to where they are, or will be anyway. He said he's been there, a lot of his friends meet their wives there on occasion because it's so beautiful. He chose it; I'm just showing up."

"Okay."

"I'll be fine."

"I know you will be. I see you are. You really are. Tom would be proud of you."

"He would. We never talked about all this, but we both agreed that life is for the living. That every day is a gift, and you have to live. You have to participate, not just hang out on the sidelines. When I said yes to Vietnam, I could see him high-fiving someone about it. Saying *there she goes, she'll be okay.* Because that's how we were. Why sit back on the sidelines when you can participate in a big way?"

"Well, you can't get much bigger than this. You're going to have fun. I'll be thinking about you."

"I know. And I wouldn't be doing this without you. You've been my rock. Always have been, always will be. You know that, right?"

"Oh, now you're just trying to butter me up."

"Of course I am. That's what little sisters do to their big brothers."

"So three weeks 'til you leave, huh?"

"Yup."

"Maybe I'll fly up next weekend; we can do dinner. I'll see if Lisa wants to come."

"That works for me. Just let me know. There's always a room for you."

"I want to meet him. You know that too."

"Of course. As soon as he gets back."

"Like immediately."

She smiled, seeing her big brother's face as he came to terms with her budding relationship.

THE WRITER

"Can we wait until he gets off the boat?"
"Okay, but just barely." He chuckled.
"I'll tell him."
"I'm happy for you."
"I know."
"I love you."
"Me too."
"'Gotta go."
"Bye."

Chapter Forty-Two

From: Kelly
Subject: I was talking about you
To: Aiden

Big brothers. Sheesh!

We talk almost every day. Sometimes it may be a quick text, but usually, we talk at least for a few minutes.

I decided it was time he knew I was leaving for Vietnam. So I called his wife instead.

Yep, still know how to play my big brother.

It took longer than I thought, a full twelve minutes before my phone rang.

Questioned me the way only big brothers can do. You okay? You're sure?

Then he let it go. That's what I love about him. He just makes sure I'm okay. I know no matter what, he has my back.

I kind of let loose on him a bit. Told him I'm done sitting on the sidelines. I'm ready to start participating again in a big way.

That's what I wanted to tell you.

I'm in. I'm ready to have a life again. I'm ready to participate.

I have no idea what that means. I just know I'm ready.

I know you'll understand this when I say I haven't thought about Tom since I said yes to Vietnam. I mean, not *really* thought about him. You know, like he's always there, in your mind, right on the tip of my tongue. Like he's still in my life.

I mentioned him to Chris. Emailed about him to you. But I haven't been attached to him. It's almost like he's taken a step back. He's fading.

And of course, I cry at writing that. But it's true.

He's fading in a good way. Because he'll always be there. But I feel like he's not here. Not in the moment. Not right now.

I have something else to think about now. My life. My movements. What I want to do next.

THE WRITER

Before it was always about what Tom and I were going to do. I just made our old dreams an extension of what I was going to do. And for the first time, I don't see it that way anymore.

It's me. What I want to do. How I want to move forward. Where I want to go. What I want to do. Who I want to be with.

Scary.

Good.

Thanks for that.

What's your favorite color?

Kelly

Chapter Forty-Three

From: Aiden
Subject: Favorite color
To: Kelly

I don't know if I have one. Depends on what we're talking about.

My cars have mostly been red.

My house has a lot of blues and greens. Kind of a beach thing going on.

I loved that purple dress you had on when I first laid eyes on you in the restaurant.

I adored that black lace you had on Saturday night.

See? Depends.

Aiden

Chapter Forty-Four

From: Kelly
Subject: Favorite color
To: Aiden

Cool.

Red. Blue. Green. Purple. Black.

Time to go lingerie shopping ...

Kelly

Chapter Forty-Five

From: Aiden
Subject: Favorite color
To: Kelly

You know you're killing me, right?

Aiden

Chapter Forty-Six

From: Kelly
Subject: Shopping
To: Aiden

Yup.

Kelly

Chapter Forty-Seven

"I can't believe you're leaving tomorrow!" Beth clung to Kelly's neck, choking her while she bounced up and down.

Kelly pried her arms away, laughing at the excitement bubbling over in Beth's eyes. "I'm not going to be able to go if you kill me." She tried to give her friend a disgruntled look, but her excitement was too much to hold back.

Kelly grabbed Beth's hands and did her own little jump-up-and-down dance. "Can you believe I'm leaving in the morning? It seemed like forever and now it's here," she squealed.

Kelly closed the door behind Beth and led the way to her living room. She had little piles ready and waiting to make their way into the suitcase.

Beth zeroed in on one. Of course. She carefully fingered the stacked lace, picking up a black and purple thong. With raised eyebrows, "Nice." And flashed her friend a wicked grin.

Kelly rolled her eyes. And giggled.

The two fell to the couch like a pair of high school kids talking about their first conquests.

"So he's there first?"

"Yep. He'll be waiting when I get there. He's going to get the car so we can leave immediately. You know, I have no idea what we're doing or where we're going, and I don't care."

Kelly went back into the kitchen, grabbed two glasses and a bottle of wine and returned to the sofa. They curled up facing each other, talking excitedly about her plans.

"You have no idea what you're doing?"

"Nope. I kind of like it that way. He sent over a couple of links to places. Asked if I liked 'this or that' kind of stuff. But other than that I have no agenda, no expectations."

Kelly filled both of their glasses and took a sip.

"You know, I've always been a control freak, having to plan everything to the nines. But I'm kind of liking this. This is all so new to me; I'm just walking into it blind. Going with the flow. Excited. That's it. I'm kind of scaring myself."

"You *have* changed. I mean that in a good way. I see some of your old bubbly self back." Beth eyed her friend for just a moment. "Yet different. I like it. I'm glad to see a happy glow in your face again."

"Thanks." Kelly reached out and squeezed her friend's hand. So much was said between them with that little squeeze.

"And are you going to glow when you get back." Beth cackled as she pushed her friend back into the couch.

"Is that all you can think of?" Kelly eyed her.

"Of course!"

They fell together, laughing, toasting to the next week.

"So what's next?" Beth said quietly.

Kelly could see a lot in that watchful eye she sent her way. She loved her friend. And she knew Beth had been there loving her, supporting her, helping her get her feet back underneath her again.

"I have no idea. Don't worry. I haven't thought much beyond this trip. I don't think he has, or at least he hasn't talked about it. We email about the past, the present. What we're doing in Vietnam. The future is always more generic terminology. I don't think either of us is ready to think that far into the future yet." Kelly took a deep breath. "One day at a time."

"So you honestly haven't thought about it?" Beth eyed her as if knew better. Her friend was a thinker; that's what she did best.

"Well, of course, I've *thought* about it. I just haven't shared it with anyone."

"And?"

"And ..." Kelly took another sip. Thought for just a moment more. "I'm keeping things open. If this goes well, we'll move forward."

"And are you hoping things go well?"

"Yeah, I am. I mean, I enjoy him. He's funny. He's charming. He's sexy as hell. I like the way he thinks. We have a ton in common. That's a great starting point, don't you think?"

Beth nodded her head in agreement. "Yeah, I suppose so. I haven't done this in twenty-five years. But it's a good place to start."

"I keep thinking back to college. We looked at life so much differently back then. Life was new. We wanted a family. To build an entire life with someone." Kelly sat up, poured more wine. "Now it's more about common interests. Finding someone that gets you, who has traveled a similar path. Someone who understands what you want. At least that's what I've concluded after these past few weeks. And with that in mind, Aiden and I have clicked."

"So how would it work?" Beth searched Kelly's eyes for clues. "Have you thought about what being together would mean?"

"I don't know. I know he's got a house in San Diego. I'm here. Neither of his girls are in San Diego; they're young. I wouldn't stay here just for Taylor; she may move as she continues to work and grow. I'm happy here. But that doesn't mean I couldn't be happy somewhere else. I've only been here three years. In any case, that's a long way off. It's not something I'll even consider for a very long time."

Kelly pulled her knees up to her chest, wrapped her arms around them. Yes, she'd thought about this a lot. Would she be willing to move? For a guy?

How sure would she have to be to do it?

"So, marriage?"

Beth brought Kelly back to reality quickly with those words.

"Wait, what?" She looked hard at her friend.

"Would you marry him?"

"No. Not now. Not for a very long time, if ever. I don't think marriage is that big of a deal anymore. Commit, yes. Marry, no. I mean, I'm not saying never. But my life is good, set. So much of my life is working right now. Why would I complicate that with marriage? I just don't see myself doing that again. But I won't say never."

"Do you think things are serious with Aiden? Are you ready to commit to more?"

"I don't know. Chris asked me that too when we talked about Vietnam. I know it's hard to understand. I don't understand it. Aiden and I've only seen each other, what, like twelve hours?" Kelly thought back to their weekend together.

"Other than that, it's all been through email. And Skype a couple of times. I've forgotten what he feels like. What he looks like. His mannerisms. His movements. We've talked a lot about that in email. This is the strangest thing I've ever been through. Him, too. So I honestly don't know what to expect." She looked at Beth expectantly. "I'm a little nervous." Kelly's eyes clouded over. "Is this crazy?"

Beth wrapped her arms around Kelly's shoulders, pulled her close. "No, not at all. I would think you're crazy if you weren't nervous."

Beth took Kelly's wine glass from her, put it down. Put her hands on her shoulders and looked her in the eye. "We've always been good girls. Married young. Had someone there for us, taking care of us. So, of course, this is all a little strange. I think so because I have Todd. Your brother thinks so because he has Lisa. You've said it many times; we can sympathize with you, but we can't empathize. And frankly, honey, I never want to. But I've watched you get through all of this, and I'm impressed with who you are today. I know I pushed ..." Beth eyed Kelly wickedly.

"Really?" Kelly smirked at her.

"And I did so for a lot of reasons. One of them being you're such an amazing person who deserves to have love in her life. I'm not saying you have to have it; I'm saying *deserves* it. You are so passionate about everything. It shines through in your books. In what you do. I mean, look at this house! It's incredible. You could turn decorating into a business if you chose to."

Kelly looked around, seeing her stuff through her friend's eyes.

Beth continued, "A person like you deserves to have passion in her life in all sorts of ways. You do well with someone close to share it with. You and Tom, you amazed me so much. You made me closer to Todd, just being with you guys. I could never have believed that old married folks could act like teenagers.

And then you two moved here, and we started hanging with you. You gave me that gift, and I can't imagine life without Todd now. I think you need that again. Not because you have to have someone. But because he would ignite your fire and keep it blazing. Keep pushing you to be who you're meant to be. You deserve that. "

Kelly felt a tear roll down her cheek. She pulled Beth close. "Thank you for that."

"It's all true."

She couldn't argue. Kelly knew that's what Tom did for her. He was always there, being her cheerleader, the one that pushed her to be her best. But she had done that for him too. That's why they'd been so good together.

"Tom was my life. I loved him like nobody's business. But I think these last twenty months have taught me that I don't need someone in my life to complete me. And Tom didn't do that. I didn't need him. I had him in my life because we met when we were so very young. And we grew together. But that's just it; we grew together where as many people grow apart. We thought alike. We acted alike. We played well together. And I loved being with him. After spending over thirty years with someone, it was almost hard to separate the two of us. I felt like we were one, you know?"

Beth nodded, knowing full well what she meant.

"But I'm strong, and I don't need that. I'm not going to settle for anything just to have a man in my life. I'm not made that way. I can do things on my own. And I have every intention of doing just that. This is about me. What I want. What's good for me."

Kelly shifted, started in again. "That said, it's nice to have someone there. To talk to. To be with. To share with. I did like that part of things. And I could do it again if I found the right person. But that's a big if. I need to move slowly. I need to think about what's best for me. And in this case, for Aiden too. This is the first romance for both of us. Slow is good for both of us, I think."

Kelly moved forward again, rested her head on her hand. "Ugh, this dating thing is even messier now than it was when we were back in school."

Beth kicked up an eyebrow as she looked at her. "You'll figure it out eventually. Maybe Aiden'll help you do it."

"Maybe. I honestly have no idea. But for now, it's fun. I'm looking forward to this. Ten days of tropical luxury in a place I've never been before? With a man I've come to like? What could be better than that?"

Beth held up her glass. "I'll drink to that."

Chapter Forty-Eight

Kelly boarded the plane early Friday morning with only one thought on her mind. Saturday: she'd see Aiden again in less than twenty-four hours.

Their countless hours of emailing had given them the opportunity to connect on a very intimate level. Yet they'd only been with each other, beside each other, for a few hours.

Still, she knew so much more about him. His goals. His desires. His past. What he enjoyed. Who he was.

Kelly snuggled down into her seat, grateful for a window. She sat back and relived the past few months. Seeing him for the first time in the restaurant. Watching him laugh as they strolled in the rose garden. Seeing his desire and control as they barely touched on the ship's deck. Learning all about him through his emails.

She sighed. And started counting down the hours.

She watched a movie. She wrote. She slept.

Would they still feel the same way when they saw each other again?

Was that small amount of time enough to know they were truly compatible beside each other?

She pushed aside her nervousness each time it crept to the forefront of her mind.

Nervousness, excitement. What was the difference?

And as the twenty-minute signal came in, her anticipation grew.

The plane landed, and she made her way into the terminal.

The airport was crowded, hot. She stood in line with dozens of other passengers from the flight, waiting her turn to go through customs. It moved faster than she anticipated, and for once she was grateful for her knack of not overpacking. She breezed through with barely a glance and found herself wheeling her way through the crowds, following the signs to baggage claim.

They'd agreed to meet there, even though she hadn't checked any. Since she was traveling light, she could quickly move around the crowds to get to her final destination.

As she approached, she began searching through the faces.

No. No. No.

And just like that, she saw him. Her breath caught deep in her chest.

He stood there, just across the terminal, old faded jeans, a tight-fitting gray t-shirt defining his chest. She'd seen his chest, knew how built he truly was. But this shirt, a simple t-shirt, accentuated every toned muscle.

She liked. A lot.

Still, he didn't see her. She moved swiftly, falling in right behind him. She snaked an arm around his waist, loving the way a simple touch brought everything into perspective. This is where she belonged, with him, right now. "You take my breath away. And at the same time, you allow me to breathe once again. How can you do that?"

She moved around him, to the front, never breaking the connection. Looked him squarely in his eyes. She brushed her lips across his, ever so softly. "I missed you."

He swept his arms tightly around her, hugged her into him as if his life depended on it. "I missed you too. I've been counting down the hours. I didn't think right now would ever come." He kissed the top of her head. "I'm glad it did."

They stood there, unbreakable for what seemed like hours. Each afraid to move and - poof - it would be over.

Finally, Kelly broke out of his hug, looked him up and down before returning to his eyes. "Do you know how sexy you are? This is the first time I've seen you in anything but your uniform." She smiled slyly up at him. "Or your birthday suit." She traced her fingers over his biceps, around his shoulders, and down his chest. "I like this shirt. It's a good shirt." She moved in and snuggled against his chest. Planted a series of kisses down his jawline.

She heard him groaning softly. He whispered playfully into her ear, "You've got to quit this, or I won't be able to move. Look what you're doing to me."

She looked back up at him. Her eyes sparkled, "Oh, I don't have to look." She took his lip between her teeth, nipping as she traced the edges.

"Kelly ..." He closed his eyes, letting the feeling wash over him.

"Yes ..." She continued kissing a trail over his jaw, down his neck. "This is going to be such a good trip." She gave him a wicked grin.

And all he could do was laugh. "A very good trip." He hugged her tight one more time. Then caught her under his arm and nudged her towards the exit. "Let's go. I need to get you to the hotel."

"In a hurry, are you?"

"You have no idea." He scowled at her. But broke out in a huge grin almost as fast. "Wait until you see this place." He opened the trunk, threw her bags in. Then pushed her against the passenger door before she could open it. He kissed her deeply, started his own journey from her ear, down her neck. Until she was breathing heavier than he.

"Aiden, I missed you so much. How far is this place?"

His eyes sizzled as he took her in. He knew just how she was feeling. He was feeling it too. "Not too far." He opened the door, helped her in.

He slid in behind the wheel, reached over, laced his fingers with hers. Softly kissed her fingers. She covered his hand with her other, rubbed her hand up his arm.

She'd never seen so much traffic, so many people. They all seemed on top of each other, fighting for what little space there was. Then a mile down the road would open up into nothing but raw beauty. It was a place like no other she'd ever been before.

Aiden pointed out some of the familiar sites he'd been to before. His previous trips had usually amounted to a weekend in the city with the guys, so he was experiencing much of the same newness as she.

The directions had them turning left onto dirt roads, right onto paths that were almost nonexistent.

THE WRITER

"Do you think this is correct?" Kelly looked worriedly as they made yet another turn.

"Steve said it was remote. Said to trust the directions, even when it appeared you were driving into nowhere." He slowed even more, worried the car was going to be eaten by a large hole.

Then the road opened up, the landscaping became more contoured, more in control. And a small sign tucked underneath a tree told them they'd found their destination.

Aiden pulled under the overhang, put the car in park and turned the key.

Kelly's eyes roamed from the resort and back to Aiden. "You're kidding." She started giggling.

He met her grin. "Nope. Come on." He met her on the other side, linked his fingers with her and walked into the open air lobby to check in.

While Aiden handled the paperwork, Kelly kept walking back towards the breathtaking view. The ocean. The flowers. The scent. She'd fallen head over heels in love with this place, and they hadn't even checked in yet.

"What do you think?" Aiden snuck in behind her, wrapped an arm around her as he pulled her close, kissed her lightly on her ear.

She was speechless. She didn't know where to begin.

He chuckled. "That good, huh?"

"Maybe, just a little."

He took her hand, led her back to the car, and parked in one of the spaces. Grabbed their luggage and gave it to their personal concierge, who led them to their private villa.

Built into the hillside on a remote section of the beach, it was water and sand as far as the eye could see. The thatched roof helped it blend into the rocks. They opened the door to pure magic. One long room was sectioned into distinct spaces. They passed through a private living space, with a glass wall that had been folded up until it disappeared. Couches and chairs inside could easily be used and enjoyed to escape the heat of the day or to stretch on after a walk on the beach or a dip in their own private infinity pool.

Through an archway, the path led to the largest, more glorious looking bed Kelly had ever seen. Miles of satin and dozens of pillows made it inviting and oh so romantic. She almost drooled thinking about what they could do on that bed. She fingered it lightly as she lingered.

She moved forward and took in the bathroom. With the glass walls folded up, the large tub for two could be enjoyed with a sense of being inside or out. The oversized shower also had an inside/outside feature that made her long desperately to stand beneath the multiple nozzles.

All in luxurious creams, whites, and soft greens and blues, it was the essence of a perfect beach retreat.

As they made their way back into the main space, their concierge disappeared and had them unpacked in minutes. He brought them each a glass of champagne and set the bottle on ice.

"If you need anything else, just push this button." He motioned to a button on the wall. "I'm Hao. I'm here for everything you need." And just as quietly, he was gone.

"Wait, he's here just for us?" Kelly looked at the space he disappeared into.

"Yep, at our beck and call."

"Hmmm. He's not too close, is he?" Her eyes blazing as she moved closer to Aiden, wrapped her arms around his neck.

He chuckled. "Somehow I think he knows when to disappear."

Their lips met, tongues tangled. Finally, alone, they fell into a rhythm, the most natural thing ever.

"I missed you. So much." She let her tongue dance across his lower lip.

"This feels so right." His hands roamed across her back, down to her hips where they settled in to hold her close.

Kelly inched her fingers down to join with his. Gently pushed him back, away from her. With a quick tug, she removed her travel clothes.

She spun, giving him a full view. "Purple. You said you liked purple."

He groaned. "It's my new favorite color."

He grabbed a hand, pulled her close. Brought her fingers up to his lips, kissed them gently.

He let his forehead rest against her. His eyes steady, looking at her as if trying to reach into her soul. "I can't believe the way I feel about you. This is crazy, right?"

"Completely." She smiled as she laced her fingers together around his neck.

As he pulled her in for another kiss, she let her hands roam through his hair.

A trail of kisses followed as he removed one strap from her shoulder, continued down.

Kelly nudged Aiden towards the bed. As she fell backward into pillows, satin, and softness, Aiden tore his jeans and shirt off before joining her in the pile.

She snuggled down. "I think I'm in heaven."

"I know I am." He fisted his hands in her hair, tipped her head just so. Their lips collided.

Devour was the only word that came to mind as she looked up at his face. All her nervousness and anticipation fell away as she discovered him all over again. She knew there was no other place on earth she would rather be.

This was where they were meant to be. To discover all there was to know about each other. To chase away demons from the past. To uncover what they meant to each other. To contemplate the future.

But for now, it was one moment at a time. One glorious moment after another as they touched, joined and connected all over again.

"Is there a reason to get out of this bed?" Kelly rolled over to snuggle in the crook of Aiden's arm. With several pillows underneath them, they had one of the most spectacular views of the ocean. The walls were folded back out of the way. The waves added to the ambiance. The gentle breeze cascaded through the room.

Several moments passed. She looked up at him, wondering if he had fallen asleep, only to discover him staring down at her. "I'm thinking."

She smiled back. Snuggled in closer. "That settles it then. I guess we'll just stay here forever."

"Works for me." He threw a leg over hers.

Entangled. Completely content. What else was there?

Kelly drifted between half-sleep and complete happiness as she felt the warmth of Aiden all around her. The early morning glow left oranges and reds dancing through their room. With a deep meditative breath, she let the quietness envelop her.

Until the rumble.

"Was that your stomach?" She pulled back staring him in the eye.

THE WRITER

With humor spreading around his eyes, he said, "What did you expect? We haven't eaten in twelve hours. If you keep working me this hard, you gotta feed me once in a while."

"Are you complaining?" She giggled.

"Nope. It's just I. Need. Food."

"Caveman talk. I know when I've been replaced." With a final kiss, she jumped from the bed.

"Should I have something delivered? Or do you want to head out and find something else?" He grabbed a menu from the side of the bed. Even though he had most of it memorized, as they hadn't left the room since they arrived.

"We've been here two days. We haven't left this little plot of paradise in two days! Granted, it's a beautiful plot of land. But maybe we should do something. Head out and see some of this city. Beyond this bedroom and that beach." She grinned at him over her shoulder as she floated naked into the shower.

Kelly loved the seclusion this place offered. An outside shower. An outside tub. Even the bed was outside when the walls were folded back, the way they'd left them for the past two nights.

As she reached for the shampoo, she felt two strong arms snake around her. "Thought I'd conserve water," he said, as he kissed his way down her neck.

She leaned into him, loving the way their bodies formed together. "This is going to postpone food a bit, you know."

"Nope. I ordered. Hao will have it here in thirty minutes." His hands captured a few of the bubbles and played with them over her skin, chased them in circles over her breasts.

She moaned and arched into him, fitting him perfectly. Her hand reached up, following his jaw behind his ear. She pulled his head down to her, took his lips between her teeth.

With a sly look, she asked, "Why Captain Maddock, whatever will we do to fill the time?"

As he continued his journey, he murmured, "I'm sure we can come up with something."

Chapter Forty-Nine

Aiden jumped out of bed, took a quick shower. If they were going to make the tour, time was ticking.

Back at the bed, he brushed his lips along her neck, pulled the covers down her body. "Hey. Rise and shine. We have to get going."

Kelly wrapped her arms around his neck. "Why? This is so comfortable." She snuggled into his neck.

He chuckled as he pulled her up and walked her towards the shower. He pushed her in and went back to get her a cup of coffee. "Forty minutes. We have to be in the lobby in forty."

They made it in thirty.

"So we're going by bus?"

"Yep."

"Why?"

"Because it's a couple of hours away."

"Why didn't we just drive there?"

"You did see the size of the potholes in the road driving up to our hotel, didn't you?"

"Yes."

"That's why. I didn't want to fight it. I figured I'd let someone else do the driving. That way I can relax and sit with you. Hold your hand. Kiss you." He took her lips between his teeth and gave a gentle tug.

"Okay." She shrugged her shoulders as she helped herself to some fruit while they waited for the bus to arrive. She feigned disinterest in their plans and watched other guests pass through the lobby. It worked for about two seconds. Then she returned her interest to Aiden.

"But where are we going?"

He loved this game. He loved playing with her. She made it so easy. Her lazy smile left him breathless as he fed into the easy banter they'd started from the moment they met.

"To a place."

"I know that. What will we do when we get to this place?"

"Visit."

"Visit what?"

"See things."

"Like what?"

"Like touristy stuff."

"Will I like it?"

"I don't know. I'd bet on it, though. That's why we're going. I figured you were getting tired of being in the room." He gave her a wicked grin as she caught his eye.

She returned the look. "Not happening. I thought we were moving there permanently!"

She wrapped her arms around his waist and pulled him in close. She was only partially kidding.

"That might be in the works."

THE WRITER

"Really?" She ran a finger over his arm that sent shivers down both of their spines.

"Maybe."

"I could live with that, you know. I'm having the best time." She held his eyes for a moment.

His eyes grew serious. "Me, too." He'd been thinking a lot about what they'd do after returning home. It was nice to know he wasn't the only one.

They linked fingers, playing a back and forth game of touching, squeezing.

Two seconds later: "So what are we doing?"

An exasperated Aiden said, "Are you always like this?" Though his eyes said he liked playing this game.

She smiled shyly. "Maybe. But only if I don't know where we're going. So just tell me, and I'll quit."

"Guess."

"Guess? How am I supposed to guess?"

"Guess."

"Museum?"

"Nope."

"Shopping."

"No."

"Hiking."

"Not exactly."

"Okay, now we're getting somewhere. We're going hiking?"

"No, not really. But you said you liked being outside. I think you're going to love this place." He pulled out his phone and opened up a file he'd been saving since she said yes. He found the photos and held it out to her.

"Wow." She turned and searched his eyes. "It's gorgeous."

"I know, right? That's what I thought."

"Are these sand dunes? And fishing boats? All of this at one place?" She scrolled from photo to photo, taking in every activity. "Kitesailing? Have you ever done that before?"

"No. You?"

"No. Though I'd love to try."

"I checked into it, but we're only there a few hours this afternoon. I didn't know if you'd like it. And it takes several hours of instruction, so we just don't have the time. I went simpler. We'll save it for some other time."

Kelly caught the hopeful way he said that. His voice said he wanted to do this again, with her. And she didn't mind it one bit. These past three days had been some of her happiest days in a long time. She didn't want it to end anytime soon.

"Deal. Some other time." She grinned. "Don't think I won't hold you to that. I'm pretty extreme when it comes to my sports."

Aiden kicked up an eyebrow. "Really? What do you consider extreme?"

She flashed him a look that said she'd try just about anything. "Ever bungee jumped?"

"No."

"I did. Twice. I grew up a tomboy, always had to keep up with my brother. My daredevil ways surpassed him years ago. He always says I'm not happy unless I'm going Mach II with my hair on fire. I ski double black diamond. Chris won't even take me to the go cart track anymore because he says I'm no fun. It's not even a close race. Plus I kinda make the twenty-something guys cry when I beat them. Skunk them. It's not pretty." She looked at him sheepishly while he laughed.

"That I'd like to see," he chuckled.

"Deal." She gave him a mischievous grin. "You'll be crying, though, as you eat my dust."

"I think I can handle it." He'd love to see her in action.

"So, back to today. No time for kitesailing? What else can we do?" She scrolled through the photos on his phone once again.

"Will a jeep tour satisfy the wild side of you?" Aiden pointed out a couple of the images he had saved. "They have red and white sand dunes. I booked a tour that covers both."

"It's beautiful."

He pulled up a few more photos. "The fishing boats come back early morning. There are the fish markets, fruit markets. We can eat all day long. We'll tour the dunes in the afternoon. Catch dinner and walk the beach. I guess the photo ops are incredible." More photos. "Sunset is supposed to be spectacular. Then we'll catch the late bus back. Sound good?"

"Perfect."

Three hours and one bus ride later, their day began.

As far as the eye could see, boats were returning home. Baskets of fish, shrimp, and scallops transferred from husband to wife, where they sorted and moved in for the sale. Aiden and Kelly walked along the beach taking in the sights and smells that came along with a fishing village.

They ate. They talked with the locals. They watched as the hustle and bustle around them kept the action constantly moving.

After lunch, Aiden and Kelly stepped into a small shop, filled out the paperwork, and followed their guide to the jeep. Buckled safely into their seats, the adventure began. And as soon as their guide learned they were adrenaline junkies, he gave them the ride of their lives. Speed became second nature as they flew from one hill to the next, pushing the limits of what the vehicle could do.

They returned tired, hot, hungry, covered head to toe in a light dusting of sand, and deliriously happy.

Arm in arm they wound their way through the busy streets back to the beach, to select a restaurant to sit, catch their breath, and inhale a meal or two.

"You're crazy; you know that, right?" Aiden laughed as they moved through the crowds.

"You were warned," she snickered. "Can you believe I got him to take that jump? I didn't know they'd do that in a jeep. I didn't see anyone else trying it. Glad we got the daredevil."

"After the first jump, even he couldn't help laughing. He was having as much fun as we were." Aiden shook his head. When she'd said she was a thrill-seeker at heart, he hadn't quite been sure what she meant. If today was any indication, he knew she was up for just about anything. He'd have to think about that and test the limits.

She grabbed his hand and pulled him into a cafe. "Here. We can sit outside and watch."

They studied the menu, ordered a few things to share, and headed outside to relax.

"Thanks. For today." With a deep breath and a heavy sigh, she gave him a satisfied smile as she nestled down into the chair.

"I should be thanking you. That was quite the adventure."

"I know, right?"

The same boats that had come in a few hours before were now being primed and prepped for another night ahead. Tourists had replaced the locals. Visitors walked the beaches, snapping pictures and buying up trinkets as they made their way across the sands.

THE WRITER

With the sunset dipping into the horizon, color spilled all around them. The red and white sands had been stunning, but the colors of the boats against the bright orange sky left them both dazed. It was a simpler way of life. And right now, simple worked.

Aiden didn't want complicated. He didn't want difficult. He'd had more "difficult" in his life and was ready for anything but.

He thought back to his last few weeks with Michelle. They'd had big plans. They'd talked about retirement. Looked forward to spending time together, just the two of them. It was something that had been so foreign for almost their entire relationship. He'd traveled so much; they'd each had weeks, months at a time where they were apart. They had too much time alone before they celebrated their time together.

They'd lived that way for most of their marriage. And it had worked. It just was. They didn't think about it. They just did it. And a part of them had worried about how they would live together, in close quarters, together every day of the year.

Yet it was something he most wanted to experience. He'd loved Michelle more than anything. To have the time to rekindle everything about them as a couple, that was what he wanted most.

He'd watched his parents grow closer after retirement. He enjoyed hearing about their latest travels, their latest ventures. He'd wanted that too. He'd wanted it with Michelle. They'd made plans.

Then cancer.

Before. After.

As they made the journey, his life became a series of before/after moments. He knew he wasn't alone. That's what cancer did to families.

Life had been good before cancer. Though he'd wondered if he really appreciated it as much as he should have.

Then after. It went from bad to worse so quickly.

Michelle knew almost from the beginning it wasn't going to be good. She talked about it. He ignored, of course. But still, she had her say. He let her talk, even though he'd tried not to pay attention, figuring he'd get his way and everything would be okay in the end.

"I want you to be happy." "You shouldn't live life alone." "It's okay if you get married again. You don't need my permission, but you have it." Suddenly, he could hear all the things she'd told him in those days they'd been cooped up in the hospital, waiting for treatments or doctors' visits.

She'd also said that life's too short, over and over again. She was right. They'd learned the hard way.

Now he faced life without her. He'd managed.

He also realized that he no longer wanted to.

He wanted the simple act of having a home with someone in it. He wanted to have someone to care about. Someone to wake up to in the morning with and lay down with at night. He hadn't realized how much he missed that, how much he wanted it again, until this trip.

This trip had taught him a lot about the woman sitting beside him. But more importantly, it had taught him about himself too.

He knew he was a married kind of guy. He'd been with someone since college. Lived with a wife and a family ever since. Some people got the whole marriage thing. Some didn't. He was one who did.

He'd had married role models his entire life. His parents. His aunts and uncles. His brother. His friends. Most of the people in his life were married, all of them strong marriages that stood the test of time, year after year.

And while he'd never thought much about it, he realized he liked that part of life. He wanted it again. Someday.

He realized it was too soon for that with anyone, Kelly included. But suddenly he could see himself doing it again. The whole wild and messy lifestyle that went along with it.

He wanted it. Possibly with her. His eyes skimmed over her, steadied on her face until she returned his gaze.

"You're staring. What are you thinking?" She reached out for his hand.

"How much fun I've had with you today."

"Funny, I was thinking the same thing." She smiled.

Aiden pulled her fingers up, kissed them before laying their hands in his lap.

"The bus leaves in an hour. Anything else you want to do?"

"Not a thing. This is perfect."

With a drink in hand, they silently watch colors dance across the sky, changing blues and grays to reds and oranges. Until finally it dipped back to shades of blue once again.

Kelly was the first to speak. "Beautiful show."

"Yep."

"It never gets old, does it?"

"Nope. There's something about the sun dipping into the water. It gets me every time. And I've seen a lot of sunsets this way."

"I imagine you have."

"It gives me hope. Makes me think."

Somehow Aiden knew this was a start, a changing point. The past was in the past, and it was time to leave it there. He'd always love everything about it. But now, it was time to look forward.

He'd have a new life. One that didn't include the Navy.

And maybe, just maybe, one that included Kelly.

She took him to places he didn't think he'd see ever again. She made him feel. She made him want. She completely did him in.

And he loved every moment of it. Couldn't wait for even more.

He stood up, held out his hand. "Ready?"

Chapter Fifty

"So what were you like as a kid? Were you the good little boy? Or were you the devil in disguise?"

Kelly peered over the top of her coffee mug with a twinkle in her eye as she waited for his answer.

They'd developed a routine in the short time they were together. When they finally rolled out of bed, Hao had breakfast ready at a table on the beach. They enjoyed the perfect blend of fresh fruits, breads, juice and coffee. They sat together and enjoyed the quiet hush of the waves as they stuffed their bellies.

Aiden narrowed his eyes. "Which do you think I was?"

"Well, I've never met your brother. But since he's the oldest, something tells me he was the good kid that got into trouble when he retaliated against something you did. I was the youngest too, you know. I got Chris into trouble all the time. It's second nature to us last-born kids." She smirked as she watched his eyes reveal she was close to the truth.

"Alex would definitely agree with you on that one. I, however, will never admit to that."

She gave his thigh a nudge with her toe.

"Come on, give it up. Give me a story, Captain. I'll never tell your Mom. I promise."

Kelly watched as he sat his mug down and went into story mode.

That's what she loved most about their relationship.

From the night in Portland where they'd first discovered each other, they'd learned how to bring moments to life and capture each other's attention with a wave of a hand and a captivating description. Aiden had said over and over again that he wasn't a storyteller, but he was sadly mistaken.

With every flick of his wrist and detailed description, he enchanted Kelly with his stories. She liked watching as he relived the highs and lows. She enjoyed the way he wove his tales together, almost being transported to different places in time.

Not a storyteller, pffft.

"Alex is three years older than me. So, of course, he was always able to do more than me. But that didn't stop me from tagging along. At one point we lived near a new construction site. Our parents told us over and over again not to go near it; it was too dangerous. But of course, that didn't stop us. He'd take his bike and balance as he rode over the beams. He'd say he could do it since he was older. I had to watch since I was too small."

"Yeah, right. You did it anyway."

"Of course I did. I'm not going to sit on the sidelines."

"He knew it, too. Wanted to get you in trouble."

"Yep."

"And it backfired."

"Yep. We weren't supposed to be there. He was supposed to be watching me. I shot off away from him, leading the way, proving I could do the same things as him. I got stuck. He tried to help." Aiden stopped and refilled his coffee mug.

"And?"

"And he broke his arm. He never told Mom it was my fault, though. He protected me."

"He broke his arm?"

"Yep."

"So what did he make you do?"

"Hmmm?" He may have said nothing, but she knew that was impossible. Not if Alex had protected him.

"Oh, come on. If he protected you, he held it over you for weeks. He scared you shitless at some point, threatening you. I know he did."

Aiden snorted.

"Am I telling this story or are you?" He sat back, watching her, as he sipped his coffee.

"We are way too much alike, you and I. If I could count all the times I got my big brother in trouble, it'd probably be in the millions. It sounds like you did the same things to your brother. You and I are cut from the same cloth. I'm sure our brothers would trade us in if they could."

"I don't know about that. It sounds like you have a great relationship with your brother."

"Yep. No complaints. Chris and I are very close. I know I've said that a lot. But I really can't imagine life without him. What about you? Are you close to Alex?"

Aiden thought for a moment. "Yes. In some ways. He's in D.C. and I'm in San Diego, though, so we don't see each other much anymore. We talk a couple of times a month if we can. Life happened, you know?"

Kelly nodded.

"In a lot of ways he's closer to Mom and Dad than I am. They all live in Maryland, so it's to be expected. Alex and Deb are good for each other. Their kids are a few years older than my girls, both married, so he's in a different spot than I am. I'd like to think that'll change once I retire."

"So your plans include spending more time back east?"

"Maybe. I don't know. About a year ago, Alex called me up and surprised me with a trip. I think it was a ploy to find out how I was doing. But I went along with it. We'd done a lot of fishing growing up, so he booked a fishing trip to Colorado. I met him there, and we spent five days sitting by the river, fishing poles bobbing in the water, and way too many beers to count."

She grinned. "Sounds like a fabulous time."

"Yeah, it was pretty spectacular," he agreed. "I'd like more of that."

They sat and looked at one another, each deep in their own thoughts.

She'd had a large support system when Tom had died. Her parents flew up every few weeks. Chris had filled in between. And when they weren't available, Beth and Taylor had done more than their fair share. Even with that much help, Kelly'd had other friends pop in and out to "surprise" her and take her out for lunch or dinner. She was loved, and she knew it.

But her friends and family were nearby. She imagined them being on the other side of the U.S., not being in her face as much as they were.

"You did a lot of it alone, didn't you?"

He knew what she was asking. That's the thing about living through grief. You knew when someone had something to say about it.

"I suppose. Not really. I mean, my mom was there for the first month. Mike's always been there. I had work."

"That's not the same thing."

He shrugged. "I got through."

"You had no choice."

"We had no choice. You were in the same boat."

"True."

"And I had support before as well. My mom was there a couple of weeks. Michelle's mom was there for a few weeks. So was her sister. Our friends brought food through a lot of the treatments. We had a lot of visits from the other couples in my unit. Everyone pitched in and did a little bit here and there."

"I always forget that. For me, it happened and then I dealt with it. But you were dealing with it for several months before and after. You had time to prepare."

"I guess that's true. Though I don't how you're ever prepared for all of that. Every day was like finding a new level of hell. It was always something. And just when you adjusted, something else happened. Honestly, I hated it when people would come in and try and help. It just always brought the reality of it all to the surface. If we were just doing our thing, it seemed to be easier. Help always meant talking about it and reliving it. I hated that."

"But it gave you a chance to talk about it. With her, I mean. You got to say goodbye in your own way. Did it get to that point? Where you said goodbye?"

She saw the hurt spread across his face. Knew it still tortured him. Yet she wanted to know.

"She did. Always. She constantly gave me these little pep talks. Live again. Be happy. Stay close to the girls. Do this. Do that. I hated that most of all." The tension in his shoulders, his face, said he didn't like to go back there. Not at all.

"Did you say goodbye?"

He scrubbed a hand over his face. He hated doing this. He'd done his best to push it aside. And here Kelly was trying to pry it back to the front of his mind.

"The last day she woke up almost happy, more relaxed than I'd seen her in days. The first thing she said to me was 'It'll all be alright now.' I asked her what she meant, and she just asked for everyone. So I rounded everyone up, and we crowded around her. She looked peaceful. She smiled. I said I love you. And that was it. It was all surreal. So fast. And yet I still see it in slow motion. In a lot of ways, it was a good experience. She was calm finally, not like she had been for weeks, tense and in so much pain."

A small sob escaped him. He paused, a tear trailing down his cheek.

Kelly gave his hands a small squeeze and let him capture his breath.

He wiped his eyes, leaned forward with his head on his hands.

"It had to be different for you. It just happened."

"I've screamed about that so many times. I never got to say goodbye. Maybe that's why I'm obsessed with it in other people. Maybe it's why I dig. Sorry about that." She felt bad, now that she'd pressed so hard.

"No. It's okay, really. That had to be difficult." Aiden tried to imagine walking in her shoes.

Once again, she reflected on the differences of their experiences. "I've often thought about what's easier, knowing or having it happen in a flash. Is it better to have the time to say goodbye, or have it happen in an instant and move on from there? Did you have it easier knowing it was coming, or did I have it easier just accepting what happened? Because that's the

THE WRITER

one thing that has bothered me the most. I never got to say goodbye. I never really made peace with it because there was still so much to say. I don't know why that's been so difficult for me, but it has."

"Trust me when I say I think they both suck. At least he was happy and healthy to the end. You enjoyed each other. You had fun. You didn't have to watch him wither away."

"True." She couldn't imagine watching Tom, who had always been so full of life, slowly fade into nothing. It that respect, she was glad it had been quick. That would have killed her, watching him lose the passion and liveliness he'd shared with her every day.

"Aiden, what are we doing here? We're reliving this again and again. It's such a beautiful day. We have to quit. We have to quit living in the past."

"It always comes back to this, doesn't it? Do you think we'll ever move past it?"

"I'd like to think we will. I don't want to keep reliving it forever."

"Do you think it's easier since we're both in the same place? We'd probably drive other people insane."

Kelly knew she cared for Aiden deeply. But at times like this, she always returned to the one thing her brother had asked her months before. *Do you think you've grown close because you're both dealing with grief at the same time?*

She knew it was more than that. She loved being with Aiden too much. But still, she wondered if that was one thing that made their relationship that much easier. The fact that he'd gone through it too.

Aiden shook his head. "I know we have this in common. But how many people our age are living this as their reality too? How many people stare down death's door as they watch their spouses leave this earth? It seems fifty is the magical age for that, doesn't it? How many people do you know that have had major health issues already? Or maybe I notice it more with everything that has happened." He could count a half dozen in a matter of seconds.

"That's true." She'd met a woman at a party earlier in the year who had talked about this very thing. It was life. It did happen. They were living proof.

Aiden stood up, pulled her up from her chair and with an arm around her waist, moved her back indoors.

She looked up at him expectantly. "Where are we going?"

He grinned. "We talk too much. We're going to share a shower and head into the city. It's time to play. You haven't seen everything this city has to offer yet. And I've got a few places I want you to see."

She smiled back. For now, she'd have to push her thoughts away. She had some living to do with the gorgeous man walking beside her. "Sounds like a perfect plan."

Chapter Fifty-One

Aiden drove slowly back into the city. He'd chatted with Hao and filled the map with circles of things to do, places to park. Now all he had to do was survive the hordes of traffic and the potholes bigger than the car.

"I'm never going to complain about California traffic ever again."

Kelly grinned as they sat and watched two men fight over what appeared to be an accident between two motorbikes.

Aiden edged out into traffic, attempting to move around. Yet without understanding how to navigate the chaos around him, he did little more than cause another obstacle. The honking and yelling pursued.

"Here. Turn at the next street. Hao has a circle off to the right. We should be able to park over there."

Grateful for Hao's directions, Aiden parked, and they made their way back to the street.

With an arm around her shoulder, they moved into the crowds. "What do you want to do first?"

The decision was made for them.

Street food was everywhere. The smells - some good, some bad - wafted up all around them.

"Try this." "Eat here." "Buy this." They were quickly overcome by the amount of people vying for their attention. They stood out, tall and fair, in this sea of likeness. Personal space was nonexistent.

Aiden pulled her to the side, and they assessed their choices. "We can eat anywhere. I've never heard of anyone getting sick from eating street food here. What's your preference?"

He waited as she looked around and weighed the options.

"Let's stay simple. You can't go wrong with noodles and vegetables, right?" She'd found a cart off to her left, and they navigated their way to it.

"You like this food?" The stranger started questioning them as they walked up to the window.

No greeting. No friendliness in her voice. Just bluntness. A question that had to be answered.

Aiden had warned her she'd have conversations like this all over town. She was actually beginning to enjoy the candor of their questions.

"Yes, we like this food very much." Together they chose a few things to sample and share.

"You'll like this?"

"Yes, we will."

"Why?"

"Because it's delicious. We enjoy it." Kelly tried to assure her as she took the first selection.

THE WRITER

"It is delicious. But most foreigners don't like it." The stranger eyed them curiously as she finished preparing their food.

"I guess we're not most foreigners. We like to try new things." Aiden smiled, giving her a nod and handing over the money.

"Where are you from?"

"The U.S. Oregon and California."

"Two places? How can that be?"

Kelly didn't want to get into their living arrangements with a stranger. She regretted being so specific.

"He lives in California. I live in Oregon." As if that would end the discussion.

"You're not married?"

"Nope."

"Soon. You should marry soon."

Aiden laughed with the stranger taking it all in stride, continued making small talk until he finished the transaction.

They stepped aside and tried to get away from the rush of the people.

Kelly took a bite, then forked a few noodles and fed them to Aiden. They ate quickly, sharing the food between them, avoiding spills as they were bumped and jostled again and again.

"Here. You have to try the soup. I think it's the best we've had yet."

"The flavors. Amazing."

Neat and tidy could never describe the process of eating street food. But both agreed it was some of the best they'd had so far. And who could spend time dawdling over a meal when there was so much to see?

Old. That was one word she would use later as she described the city. She began accumulating them in her mind for when she returned home. Wild. Chaos. Friendly. Modern in a weird sort of way.

The most thrilling experience of her life.

She didn't care where Aiden led her. She was merely along for the ride. Grasping his hand as he pulled her along, in and out of destinations, stopping to have strange and surreal conversations with many of the people around them.

She laughed. She thoroughly enjoyed.

She never wanted to leave.

Still, after another street meal late in the evening, they both admitted it was time to go.

"I'm not sure I can make it back to the car. I think my shoes are stuck permanently to my feet. And I smell even worse. Did you see what I stepped in back there?" Kelly shuddered at the thought. She'd known it was bad the minute she felt it squish up the sides of her shoes and onto her feet.

"I'll pull them off of you before you get into the car."

He'd done exactly that as he lifted her up, swung her into the car, tugged them off, and threw them into the trunk, before settling in behind the wheel.

"I'm going to need a shower before I get into bed." She sat staring at her feet. She dabbed at them with a couple of napkins she had found, tried to keep the muck off the floor mats. She wondered if she'd ever get them clean.

He tried to hold his composure. But the smell ... He finally cracked, rolled the window down and cackled as he saw the look on her face. "Did you have fun?" He grabbed her hand and pressed her knuckles to his lips.

She grinned ear to ear. "The best."

The drive back to the hotel was even more intimidating after dark.

Aiden concentrated on the road, the traffic. Kelly studied him.

She traced over his face with her eyes, over his shoulders, down to his arm resting in her lap.

She captured his fingers with hers. He felt so good. He felt so right.

Scary? Yes. In a very delicious way.

She sank deeper into his warmth, his strength.

Content for the moment to be near him, touching him, watching the darkness zip by. With only the hum of passing traffic from a half-opened window, the questions flowed.

What now?

What would they do when Aiden returned home?

Would they try and make it work?

Was this what she wanted?

What about him?

She'd fallen for Aiden; she'd known it from the start. But what did that mean?

Tom had been her everything. She loved every moment of being with him. Sure, they'd had a few bumpy patches along the way; what marriage didn't? Still, they'd stuck it out, working through the rough parts until they'd turned it around once again. It was life. A normal marriage. With highs and lows, good and bad. And she'd loved him, desperately so.

But she'd been so young when they'd fallen in love. They lived together and were married soon after college. She'd never had a life on her own. And as much as she loved being a couple, she found herself enjoying being a single for the first time in her life.

Beth may have harassed her into finding a new relationship. And she was grateful; she'd loved every moment she'd spent with Aiden. But did she want this again permanently, so soon? To have a man in her life twenty-four hours a day? Being there, worrying about her, following her movements, helping her even when she wanted to do things on her own?

She'd learned so much about herself in these past couple of years. And as much as she loved being married, she found she really enjoyed being single too.

Could she have both? Could she enjoy her time alone as well as having time together? Could they make this work in two separate cities? At least for a while?

This was so new to her. Him too. And as much fun as she knew they were having together, she knew she wanted to take it slow. To make sure this was right. To make sure this was something that worked for the both of them, together.

After all, there was a lot of blending that would have to occur to make it work. Two houses. Two families. Two cities. Two personalities. Two lifestyles.

It was working well here in paradise. But that didn't mean they wouldn't face trials and tribulations when reality moved into place. That's when the true test would occur. She didn't want to rush into anything. She didn't want to make a mistake and cause herself any more pain.

She'd experienced more than enough pain in her life. If taking it slow would help her figure that out before she made a mistake, she was willing to take it slow.

She glanced at Aiden one more time as they made their way up the driveway to the hotel. She adored him. She possibly even loved him. But she wanted to make sure they worked on every level before she moved forward in a big way.

Still, they had now. And for now, she loved every moment of their time together. And she'd continue to enjoy it until the moment they stepped on the plane once again.

She wrapped around his arm, drew out his warmth, grasped his hand a little tighter. He was all hers for now.

Aiden parked outside of their villa.

He made his way around the car. Held his hand out to pull her out of the car. "Give me your hand. I'll carry you. I'll get your shoes in the morning."

"I can walk," she said as she stumbled on a rock.

With a raised eyebrow and a knowing look, he swept her up into his arms.

She laced her fingers around his neck and held on.

"I think I might have to throw my shoes away. I'm not sure I'll get this off of my toes."

He deposited her into the shower, where she peeled off her clothes and began the tedious chore of making her feet respectable once again. Four rounds of scrubbing later, she emerged from the shower donned in a bathrobe. And took her first look around.

Of course, it was perfect. Hao made sure of that. Even after just a few days there, they wouldn't have expected anything else. The breeze silently flowed through the room. The pillows fluffed just so. The covers tucked down, inviting them in. Even a few flowers in a vase on the nightstand. And standing on the patio, looking out at the ocean, was a man who took her breath away yet again.

She could see just the silhouette of his shape, standing just out of reach from the soft glow of the light by the bed. He held one glass of champagne to his lips, drinking, with another down by his side. Waiting, for her.

She snuck in behind, wrapped herself around him. Took the glass and drank as she followed his gaze.

They stood there watching, listening, feeling each other.

Their last night.

No words were spoken. Between them, they each had so much to say.

But where to begin?

So they did what came naturally.

He took her glass, put them both on the table beside him.

Captured her fingers in his, holding on tight.

She wrapped her arm around him, snuggling into his neck. Gently nibbling and tasting.

His hands traced over her back. Moving lower on her spine.

Then he dipped down, capturing her mouth with his own.

While tongues tangled, they worked buttons and zippers.

Then mirrored each other as they fell silently to the bed.

Rising above her, Aiden fisted his hands in her hair. Searching, his eyes roamed freely over her face, down her body and back again.

"Stunning," he whispered.

Then moved, slowly down. Kisses. His tongue traced down each delicate inch, nibbling deeper while she sighed and caught her breath.

"I could really get used to this," he mumbled into her skin, licking and blowing to make her shiver with anticipation.

"This good?" His hands traced over her thighs, settled between. His fingers found where they were meant to be. Slowly moving, back and forth. In. In deeper.

She moaned.

THE WRITER

He smiled. "I'll take that as a yes." He continued his journey.

He loved going slow. Slow made her pull into him. Slow made her breathe wildly, scraping her fingernails down his back.

Slow made time stop.

There was no place on earth he'd rather be.

He drove her wild, making her buck underneath him until he could feel how truly close she was.

She placed a hand on each side of his face and they locked eyes.

"I want you. I want this. Us. It's so good." She pulled him back up to capture his mouth in her own.

She slid her hands down his back. Found him. Gently guided him.

They found their rhythm almost immediately.

With a hand on each hip, she rocked up into him with every move he made. Reaching him. Finding him. Moving closer to him.

She could feel it in his tempo, heard it in his breathing.

Close, she moved, letting him touch her deeper. She wanted nothing more than to go to their secret place ... together.

He looked into her eyes, watching. He anticipated. He touched. He wanted to fall together, with her.

And just like that, he knew.

"I love you."

She knew he felt it. She could see it in his eyes.

And in some ways, she felt it too.

She stared deeply into his eyes. Captured his lips.

She'd never thought about finding something like this again. She still wasn't sure if she wanted it, not all the way.

In a short period of time, he'd become her world. He supported her. Cared for her. Shared in her dreams. Gave her things she'd only recently decided she wanted again for herself. He thought of her and showed it in his unique way.

She could see feeling pouring out, spilling from his eyes. She could hear it in the three simple words he'd softly said. She could feel it in the way his fingers tenderly caressed her skin.

But was this it? If she said the words, would that seal the deal? Did she mean them? Or would "I love you" be saying too much too soon?

It was more than she had to give, right here, in the present.

Instead, she melted into him. She gave him her all.

It would have to do for the moment. It was all she could give. For now.

Chapter Fifty-Two

Aiden moved to the side. She saw it in his eyes. Felt it in the way he pulled away from her almost immediately.

He rose. Made his way to the bathroom.

She followed just as quickly.

"Aiden."

"Give me a minute."

He closed the door tight.

She paced back and forth, trying to put the words into formation. She wanted to say the right things, to make him understand.

To take away that terrible, horrible look she'd seen in his eyes for just a moment.

Finally, he opened the door. And pushed by her, back into the room, back to the stairs that led to the beach. He sat down heavily, breathing deep, soaking up the smell of the air. The beach was his comfort. The sand, the salty air, his serenity. And right now he needed all he could get.

Kelly dropped beside him, moving in to capture his attention. "Aiden. Look at me. We need to talk."

"Really, there's nothing to talk about. Obviously, we aren't on the same page here. I didn't see that coming, but it's good to know before we leave here in a few hours." He'd give anything to be able to run. But darkness presided over the beach, with just a sliver of moon to light the way. He wasn't going anywhere.

"Aiden, I want to talk about this. I want to explain …"

He cut her off. "No, you don't need to say anything."

She continued, "Yes, I do. Because it's not what you think."

Once again, she saw the hurt in his eyes. And it made her that much more determined to make sure this was right before they committed in a bigger way.

He tried to get up. He tried to walk away. But she held strong.

"You told me you loved me. Did you mean it?" She knew he did. His eyes gave him away, even now.

"Of course I meant it. I wouldn't have said it if I didn't mean it." His voice was sharper than he would have liked it. But he used it to try and cover up his pain.

She held his eyes, holding his hands to keep him settled. "Where do you see this going?"

"Honestly, I have no idea. I had a great time this week. I guess I got carried away thinking we both felt it. I wanted more." He stopped. "But this isn't all about me. This is about you too. And obviously, we don't see eye to eye," he said with a pointed look.

She took a deep breath. She met his eyes. And with a deep breath she began. "I adore you. Do I love you? Possibly so. But here's the thing. I've just been through this whirlwind, coming up from the bottom of thinking I wanted to die, to having a

THE WRITER

friend pestering me about giving dating a try again, to finding someone that's made my heart do flip-flops for the first time in a very long time. I've enjoyed getting to know you. I've loved exploring who we are together. This trip has been so incredible, even more than I ever expected."

He wiggled. She just pressed her hands to his face to keep his vision in place. She needed his attention, demanded it with a firm grip.

"But that's just it. It's been a whirlwind. What does us mean? We've never been in the same city to see how we'd live together. Everything we've done has been through email. And vacationing together isn't living together. I have a life in Portland. You have a life in San Diego. We need to discover who we are together in the real world. When we're *both* living in a home in the city - not on a boat half way around the world. What do we look like when we're two normal people in San Diego and Portland? How do we go back and forth? Where do we live? *How* do we live?"

Was she the only one questioning everything? He seemed like he was sure about everything. Ready to move forward. Even now, with all she'd thrown at him, he had a look that said he didn't quite get it.

So she continued. "This trip has made me realize I need to work on me just a little bit more. I need *me* back before I can give *me* to anyone. And that includes you. I need to finish letting go of my past. I need to let Tom out of my life. I need to separate my life with him, and give myself a life with just me. And only then will I have *me* to give to someone else. You. Does that make sense?"

"So this is it? You need to work on you. So what, this has been good times and then move on? What is it that you think we did here? What do you want, Kelly? Because obviously we don't see things the same way."

"I think we do." She moved in a little closer. Got into his face. "I just think you've moved a little faster than me. What's the rush? This has all been so fast. And I don't want to make a mistake with this. What if we get back to life, back to our routines in the States and find we don't work well together? Aiden, this is a big commitment. We have separate lives. We have families. We have ..."

As much as she didn't want to say it, she couldn't help but let it fall from her mouth. "Because, I like my life. I don't want to speed it up and jump into something I'm not ready for. We still have a lot to work through."

"Like what?"

Could he really not know? "Like everything. Two houses. Two lives. I still have my husband's clothes in the guest bedroom, for God's sakes." She pulled her hands away and let her head fall to his shoulder. *Why did this all have to be so confusing?*

He was silent. And when she looked back up, she could see the sheepish look spread across his face.

"You too?"

He nodded. "Still in the master closet. I haven't had time to go through everything. I've been away a lot and never made it a priority."

"See?" She pushed into him with her hands. "That's what I'm talking about. We have to work through all of that first."

Suddenly, she didn't want to talk about it anymore. She wanted to backtrack, to move back the hands of time just a bit, to when they were just on vacation, enjoying each other, not trying to decipher the rest of their lives.

She looked out at the water, wishing it were that easy.

But because it wasn't, she got up and took a few steps towards the beach.

He mirrored her, grabbed her hand and walked in silence for a while.

He loved her.

And she knew if she would admit it to herself, she loved him too.

But did she want everything that came along with it?

She stopped. She turned towards him, leaned into him once again.

"This was the right thing for me to do. You were the right thing for me. You've done more to my life than anyone could possibly imagine. You've touched me in so many ways. You've twisted my heart and made it whole again. I'm such a better person right now for having met you. You've tilted my world. You've given my hope and strength and so much more. And yes, Aiden, I probably could say those three little words to you. But they wouldn't change the fact that this is a first for both of us. We can't both jump into a relationship after having everything ripped apart as it was, we can't move forward with us without thinking about this thoroughly. I need that time. We need that time. Because when I say those three words to you, I want them to mean everything. I want to use them and have you realize they mean everything. I won't give them to you unless I can say them and truly mean them. With all of my heart."

He nodded. He heard her. He did. A part of him understood. But he had his opinion too.

"And that's where we're going to have to disagree. I'm ready, Kelly. I may have never done this before, you may be the first person since my wife, but I know what I want. I'm not willing to sit on the sidelines. I want more. I want someone in my life again. Maybe even a wife. I do. It's what I want. It's what I'm looking for. It's what I'm reaching for. I'm ready. The rest is trivial. I'll clean up the house when I get home. I'll move forward because I've made the decision to do just that. It's time. I'll be home in a few short weeks. And at that point, I want more. I'm ready, and I want it to be you. But we have to both want that."

Kelly drew in her breath, just a little. "You're ready; I get you want someone in your life. But a wife? Really? How can you even know that? Because there's no way I'm even ready to think about that again, if ever. To be honest, I'm just wrapping my head around the idea of having someone else in my life. But permanently?" She tried to hide the shock from her face.

"I don't mean now. And no, I'm not even remotely ready for that. But still, I'm not going to say no. I've realized this week that I like the idea of marriage. I like all that it brings. And I'd be lying if I said I didn't want it again at some point in the future."

A tiny piece of Kelly's heart fell away. She heard him. She knew it took guts to say what he had said. She'd love to say it too. But with everything she'd been feeling the past few days, she wasn't sure if she could.

No matter what it meant, she knew she had to stay true to her heart, slow down, take her time.

It's not just what she wanted; it's what she needed. And she wasn't going to make a big mistake by speeding up the process.

"You got everything?"
"Yep. You?"
"Yep."

THE WRITER

They were avoiding the very large elephant in the room, and they both knew it.

How did you walk away knowing you wouldn't see each other for a long time? How did you move forward when you didn't know what that meant? How did you leave when you didn't know what you were leaving? Was it for good? Could they find each other again? One thing was for sure; serious talks were out for the foreseeable future.

They drove to the airport in silence, fingers entwined, holding on.

The rental car attendant checked them in, drove them to the main terminal.

They made their way to check-in, through customs, through security.

With gates only a short distance apart, they found a quiet corner to wait. With Kelly leaving first, she watched the time click quickly by.

Kelly wrapped her arms around his waist. Put just enough distance between them to memorize his face one more time. Every line, every movement, she'd take back with her to remember over and over again in the coming weeks.

"So September, huh?"

"Not that far off."

Aiden scrubbed a hand over his face, pulled her closer for a moment. No matter how much tension was between them, no matter what was said, he knew he was in love with her. He'd have to think about that, but he knew it wouldn't change. "Can we meet when I'm back?"

"Of course, I wouldn't have it any other way." She reached up and kissed him gently. "I'll email you."

She smiled. That's where it all started. With a few simple emails. And it led to so much more.

She loved him; she knew she did. She'd bitten her tongue a hundred times, fighting not to say it, not to use it to smooth things over. But that wouldn't be fair to her or him. When she said it, IF she said it, it would mean everything. Or she wouldn't say it at all.

It'd have to wait. And if saying it changed everything, she'd have to live with it. She was going to do what was right for her. She was going to do what was right for them. And that meant getting her life in order, so she'd have it to share completely with someone else. Whatever that meant.

One more hug. One more kiss.

Kelly had thought about this moment since the day she said yes. She knew this day would be a changing point in their lives. This would be decision time.

She knew it would be difficult. Yet she hadn't realized how much. As she stood looking into his eyes, knowing they both wanted more, she contemplated how long the next few weeks would be.

She wanted this. She wanted this man. She wanted more time with him to explore.

She also wanted to think. What was next? What did the future hold? How much would they have to change to accept each other in this new lifestyle? What would those changes mean to her current life? Her family? Her daughter?

She missed what she had with Tom. Missed the familiarity of being with someone forever. Their lives were so entwined; it was impossible to see where one began and the other ended.

She knew it was the same for Aiden.

Yet here they were, trying to build a bridge and bring that same feeling together into their lives. With weeks alone until they were together again, they both had some thinking to do.

THE WRITER

But today was today. And for now, her heart ached at the thought of leaving him once again.

They called her flight. It was time for her to board.

"I'll see you on email." She smiled.

"I'll be there."

"I'll miss you."

"I'll miss you too."

He kissed her one last time.

Then he watched as she stood in line, made her way down the jetway. Then made his way to his own.

Chapter Fifty-Three

Kelly had a problem to work through. The conflict almost tore her in half.

She liked him. Loved him, even. She'd said as much a few hours before.

She knew it was true. She really did love him. But as much as that excited her, it scared the hell out of her too.

Kelly could see it in his eyes; he was ready to move a lot faster than she was. Maybe it was because he'd had the chance to say goodbye to the love of his life. Maybe it was because he was used to having a wife at home waiting for him. Maybe it was because he was used to having a long distance relationship.

But she wasn't. And she wasn't sure she wanted it now.

She truly loved Tom more than anything. They'd had the best love affair. She'd said it over and over to Chris and Beth, and she truly meant it. She'd loved Tom. He'd been her everything.

That was gone. She'd been getting over that, slowly. And she didn't want to replace it just for the sake of having someone else in her life.

She'd let herself move forward and kiss someone, have the intimacy she'd discovered she still craved. That had taken eighteen long months to work up to that point. It happened, and she'd been ready for it. She loved what Aiden did to her. Yes, she loved him.

But was it enough to change her life for him? That she didn't know.

And she wasn't willing to do that at this point. She needed more time. A lot more time.

They lived in different cities. She was just getting used to life on her own. She'd been on her own for the first time ever, and she wasn't sure she was ready to give that up quite yet.

She'd finally grown comfortable with being her own woman. To set her own rules. To decide when and where she did things. It was all her now. Nobody else. And she was having a good time with that, dammit.

Did she really want to fall back into the same pattern of having someone else in her life to dictate what she did? To watch out for her? To care for her?

She'd had that forever. She was just realizing how ingrained that had been in her life. It was nice not having that watchful eye always there.

And men did that. It was their nature. She got that. And she liked it, to a point.

Tom had done it. Even Chris did it when they were together. Aiden picked it up the moment they became something more in the restaurant. She felt it when he laid his hand on her back, guiding her through the door. She heard it when a note of worry crossed over his voice, offering to walk her home.

THE WRITER

She wasn't a little girl; she knew how to protect herself. She liked going out and doing as she pleased, without someone there to worry about her.

Then she saw Aiden's face in her mind. The slight tilt of his head. His eyebrows scrunched together. The concern in his eyes. "You'll be okay?"

That was part of being a couple. Having someone at home watching out for you, waiting for you. Worried if you didn't show up as planned.

God. She covered her eyes with her hands and breathed deep. She was going crazy, truly. *Get a grip, girl.*

Her thoughts kept spinning. Back and forth. From one thought to the next. Through every conversation.

She had a problem to work through, and she knew just how to do it.

She'd been doing it for years. She's write. That's how she solved things. That's how she worked through what was deep inside. Because even though they were all about her characters, she could try out different paths and use them to work through her own problems. That's what had made *Finding Love Again* such a success.

Nineteen hours.

Kelly had nineteen hours until her flight landed in Portland.

She settled into her seat and waited for takeoff.

People reflected back on a great trip in many ways. Some sifted through photos. Some sat in reflection. Kelly wrote. Always had. Always would.

She'd journaled throughout her life. She'd started in her youth. She had journals all through school. She'd created memory books when they started a family. But now, as a writer, she did it all the more.

In ten days, she'd changed her life for good. She knew that deep in her heart.

They'd touched. They'd connected. They'd fallen in love in more ways than one. But what was she going to do with all of that?

Kelly moved her fingers over her lips, remembering the tingle he'd placed there time and time again. He really had great lips. Knew how to use them, too.

Her mind drifted back to the moment they met.

Coincidences.

Serendipity.

Chance encounters.

Fate.

All of it was so remarkable; she still couldn't believe it was real.

What if Aiden's ship hadn't been selected for Fleet Week in Portland?

What if she hadn't said yes to Beth, met her at the restaurant?

What if they hadn't chosen the same restaurant? After all, there were hundreds in the city.

What if Beth and Mike hadn't left them alone?

What if they hadn't talked about their pasts, discovered their tragic connection?

What if they hadn't taken a chance and agreed to email each other, discover their interests, their personalities, their secrets?

What if he hadn't invited her to Vietnam? What if she hadn't said yes?

She wouldn't be sitting here, right now, at this very moment, contemplating the rest of her life. Not in quite the way she was doing right now.

THE WRITER

Of course, it all started with tragedy. And no matter how happy she was at this moment in time, she knew she'd turn back the hands if it were possible, do anything to have Tom beside her again.

Just like Aiden would have Michelle.

But that could never be.

And that was why it was time to move on.

The next fifty years were ahead of her. And it was time to live them.

It was time to recognize this happenstance moment for what it was. It was meant to be.

That thought filled her, consumed her. Almost as it had done a few months after losing Tom.

The words were there. She could see them. Could feel them. She felt the story bubbling up inside of her.

When the plane leveled at cruising altitude, Kelly opened her computer and started writing. She opened up a new file and wrote the very first words of her new book.

Chance Encounters.

A great title. An even better story.

In two hours, she had her characters profiled, her scenes arranged, the details mapped out, and the outline in place.

And from there, *Chance Encounters* took on a life of its own.

Her characters came to life, inspiration pouring into them with every stroke of a key.

And so it began.

Chapter One.

Jennifer Moore fixed her tight little skirt. Touched up her red lipstick. Glanced at her favorite Jimmy Choo's.

Okay, they may have been a bit much for navigating an airport as big as Heathrow. Still.

If fate were going her way today, she'd be damned if she was going to look anything but perfect. And that meant her favorite skirt, her bright red lips, and her beloved pair of shoes.

She navigated through customs. Wheeled her bag between other travelers searching for their gates.

She checked her ticket. Twenty-four B. On this big of a plane, what were the chances she'd even see him? Sit by him? Next to impossible.

But fate sometimes works in mysterious ways. That she knew. She'd seen it happen before.

If luck had anything to do with it, she'd see him.

If serendipity came into play, he'd be here.

Dane Masters captured her attention from the moment he'd appeared in front of her, as if out of nowhere.

He made a promise. Said nothing would keep him away.

He'd be here.

And she believed.

Nineteen hours later, over twenty-five thousand words in the file, eighteen chapters fully written, Kelly hit save one more time and closed her laptop. She tucked it into her bag and waited for the plane to land and the doors to open.

And instantly her reality set in. Her own chance encounter. The serendipitous moment when she met him, Aiden.

The love of her life as she moved forward.

Could she say that? It still felt awkward. After all, the love of her life had always been just one. Tom.

THE WRITER

Yet here Aiden was, in her thoughts. And more importantly, in her dreams. Her dreams of the future. Her dreams of what was yet to be.

She saw him, there beside her in the coming months.

It wasn't sealed in stone. Not yet. But she did see him in her future.

Aiden had a way about him that she adored. The way he touched her. The way they laughed together. Who they were becoming.

And it was coming together so quickly. Much faster than with Tom.

But, she guessed, that was to be expected.

At fifty-three, she knew who she was. She understood what she wanted out of life. She knew what she liked and what she didn't.

They were more settled. They were who they were.

Aiden got her. She got him. That was the first step. The huge hurdle that gave them a chance.

They'd passed. For ten days, they tested. Again and again. And it worked.

And now life would never be the same.

She caught the light rail to Portland's City Center, watched the city go by as she daydreamed.

Thoroughly spent, thoroughly energized, she wanted nothing more than to drop into her bed.

And start counting down the days.

August was the peak of perfection in the Pacific Northwest; the day didn't disappoint. Blue sky, perfect temperatures and tourists all around her, she pushed her way out of the bus at her stop and made her way through the streets towards her home.

She loved Portland, thought of it as her home. Even in just a few short years, she'd fallen in love with its quirkiness. She loved her condo. Loved being close to her daughter.

Was all that about to change?

A feeling of restlessness suddenly flooded her.

She had a lot to think about. Cleaning to do. More writing to complete. A business to continue to grow.

And a life to change for good. One way or the other, she had a lot of reinventing to do. It was time to break free, let go of the past, move towards a future. It wasn't clear. It wasn't written in stone.

But for the first time she saw she was on the right path. A new path.

And Aiden was there. She knew he was.

She just needed the time to put everything in its proper place. That's what she did. It's how she worked. It's who she was.

Aiden. San Diego.

It could work. It could definitely work.

She rode the elevator up to her home, to a life where significant changes were coming, soon. What that meant, she wasn't quite sure. But she was ready to give it a try.

Chapter Fifty-Four

Kelly could hear Chris fumbling with the phone. "'ello?" in a voice that was barely there.

"Hi." She chewed on her lower lip, wanting desperately to have her big brother tell her everything was going to be all right.

Panic sounded in his voice as he said, "Are you okay?"

Shoot. Kelly looked at the clock, realized what time it was. Just because she was up didn't mean the rest of the West Coast was.

"Sorry, I didn't even look at the time. Jet lag." As if that said it all.

"Jeez, Kelly. It's almost one. Give me a minute."

She heard Chris rustle around, undoubtedly moving out of his bedroom and down into the kitchen.

She sat quietly, thinking, while waiting for him to talk.

"Okay. I'm here. You made it back, how was it? I've been thinking about you."

Kelly had so much to say, yet somehow didn't know where to begin. Still, she'd been the one to call.

"I got back a few hours ago. Cleaned everything up, filled up my cupboards, wrote a little." Then with a tiny sigh, "I can't sleep."

"Time difference or too much on your mind?"

"Probably a little bit of both."

"So? Talk." She could hear the sleepiness in Chris' voice. She knew he was hardly in the mood for guessing games. She'd probably pulled him from a deep sleep. He was no stranger to being woken up. It was his life as a doctor. Whether on call or not, she knew he preferred to be notified if one of his regular patients had an emergency. As such, he received phone calls at all hours of the day.

Kelly also knew his language well. *Talk* meant spill it all. She had no problem with that. She needed him as her sounding board once again.

So she started the only way she knew how. "It was good. It was great." She stopped, murmured under her breath.

"Who am I kidding, it was fucking fantastic. God, Chris, it couldn't have been more perfect. From the moment I got off the plane, we did everything right. We spoke the same language. We got each other. Really got each other, you know? I felt myself sinking into him when I first saw him at the airport, and that feeling never let up. It's like I've known him forever. And then I fucked it all up."

She let out a little gasp at the thought.

"Okay," Chris said slowly, not sure of what to say. He gave her a moment to catch her breath. He needed a moment to focus.

"You okay?"

"Yes. No. I don't know. Chris, I'm so confused. Is this real? Can I really be feeling this way? And what the hell did I do?"

She'd give anything if her big brother were right there, sitting in front of her, telling her exactly what to do.

And somehow he picked up on that. Maybe because that's what he'd always done.

"Baby, take a deep breath." He waited and listened.

"Better?"

"Yes."

"Now we can talk. So let's start at the beginning."

And so she did.

She began her story with a tale of weaving her way through the airport, finding out nothing had dulled her feelings for the man she'd met by chance on a warm June evening. She shared their travels, their meals, the view of the ocean, their walks along the beach. And …

"And then he told me he loved me." She let that hang in the air.

"And you said …"

With an exasperated, guttural sound, she said, "Nothing. I said nothing. It didn't go well from there."

"I see." He bit back the urge to lecture her. Instead, chose to let her think and figure it out for herself.

"Why do I have to make this decision right now?" She said it with a little more anger and nervousness than she'd planned.

"You don't. You can go as slow as you need to. This was a good first step. There'll be other guys."

"No, Chris. We didn't leave on bad terms. We just didn't leave on good terms. We just … left. I have no idea what we're doing." She huffed out a breath. God, what she wouldn't give to have a relationship with someone she could visit in person or at least call on the phone.

"One question, okay?" He waited for her to answer.

"Okay," she responded hesitantly.

"Do you love him?"

"I don't know," she said weakly.

"What?"

"Dammit, Chris, I don't know."

"What do you mean, you don't know? Because it's a simple question. Do you love him or don't you? You shouldn't have to think about it. You either do or you don't."

"That's not the point."

Chris wasn't about to give up. "Kelly, do you love him?"

She sucked in a deep breath, blew it out. Then, very quietly, "Yes."

"What?"

"Yes, I do. I love him."

"Then why are you so angry about it? Why didn't you tell him?"

And the tears started to flow.

So Chris did what he always did. He let her cry.

She cried for everything. Everything she'd been. Everything she'd had. Her past. Her life. Tom.

But somewhere in the mess, she saw more. Her past began blending with her future. Her sadness morphed into happiness. Her life became more than memories. She suddenly found herself desiring to blaze new trails. She was scared and gleeful all at the same time.

Minutes later she continued. "Sorry."

"Feel better?"

"Maybe. Just a little."

"Good. So you're in love with him. And the feeling's mutual."

"Yes. Or it was until I fucked it all up."

"I sincerely doubt if you fucked it up that badly. If he loves you, a little hiccup won't stand in the way."

"You think?"

"I know."

Chris let that soak in for just a moment.

"I really gotta meet this guy. You know that, right?"

Kelly laughed. "Chris. I'm fifty-three years old. You don't have to approve everyone I meet, you know."

"Sure I do. I still know what's best for you." Chris snickered, clearly enjoying the humor that had returned to her voice. "Now, let's get down to the nitty-gritty here. You love him. He's home here in a few weeks. Then what?"

"Ugh. I have no idea. We didn't get very far after our fight. We didn't end in the best of spirits."

"Did you say goodbye or walk out?"

"I would never walk out. It wasn't that bad." *And ... yeah.* "You're a jerk, you know that, right?"

"I didn't say a word." He snickered.

She heard.

"So you said goodbye? Agreed to see each other when he gets back into town? Said you'd think things through? What?"

"All of the above. I told him I needed time to think about all of this. I needed to think about me, us, our future. I needed time to put Tom behind me. Tom's clothes are still in the spare bedroom, you know. I need time to come to terms with all of this. I don't want to rush into anything. I'm not going to make huge changes right away. I need slow. I need to think things through. I need this to be about me for a while. Not that I don't want him in my life; I do. But ..."

Kelly sat back, exhausted from thinking too much. No matter how many times she thought all of this through, the answers weren't there. She didn't know how to make it better between them, but wasn't willing to give up on herself in order to move forward. She wanted time. *Was that really too much to ask for?*

"Kelly, I'm not an expert here, but I don't think any of that is unreasonable, is it? You want time to think. He needs time to get back to his house. You need a little closure from burying your husband and moving Tom out of your life. You don't have to jump fast. A few weeks or even months shouldn't matter that much, should it?" Chris waited for an answer.

"No. It shouldn't be, right?" *So why had Aiden pushed and said he was ready for love again?*

"Is it possible you both want the same things, only you're saying it differently? You both want to move forward. You both are in. You just need to come to terms with the details. And it's hard to do that until you find out what they actually are. It's even harder to do that when it's impossible to be face to face. How long until he's home?"

"End of September."

"Can't you plan something then, when he gets home?"

"Yes. I'll be in San Diego a week later for the romance association convention. I'm keynoting."

"There you go. Plan around that. Maybe you can stay. Yes?"

"Maybe."

Chris knew his sister well. He knew she was trying to put all the pieces together, to have things settled long before she'd made up her mind to anything else. She wanted to know how she'd fit in someone else's life. Particularly when that someone lived over a thousand miles away.

"You know this has been done before, right? People have long distance relationships all the time. It can be done. It can work."

THE WRITER

"I know that. But how? How does it work? Where do we begin?" That's the part she kept getting stuck on. She liked things neat, in order. She liked a balanced life. Chaos was not her friend. And right now, that's all she could see: the pure chaos of trying to blend two lives that were so well planned out up until this point. How were you supposed to bring together two people with two different backgrounds, two different families, two different approaches to life?

"You're just overthinking this. Which is understandable, considering it's *one o'clock in the morning.*"

"I said I was sorry."

"I know. Just have to give you shit. I'm not on call tonight. I was *sleeping.*"

"Geesh, wake a guy up, and he won't let you forget it."

She loved bantering with her brother. It comforted her. Calmed her down. Helped her think a little clearer. And right now it's the one thing she needed desperately.

"I'm happy for you. More than you know." Chris managed to get the words out with only a small catch in his voice. He knew how difficult it had been for her, letting Tom go and moving forward. He'd been doing it in his own way, too. Losing his best friend was difficult. But watching his sister lose everything had been almost unbearable. To hear her coming back, finding happiness, put it all in perspective. He was desperately happy for her. So he did what only he could. What he'd been doing since they were little kids. He took charge, moved her forward in a way only she could appreciate.

"Chris?"

"Yes?"

"It's okay? I mean, it's time, right?" A part of her, a tiny part of her, still felt like she was betraying her best friend. She knew it was ridiculous. But the feeling was still there. And it wasn't something she could ask anyone else. She knew she'd get a straight answer from the one person that had been there supporting her, cheering her from the moment her life changed forever.

"It's time, baby."

They sat in silence for just a moment while Chris contemplated his words carefully.

"There isn't a magic pill you can take to make you feel better. There isn't a perfect time to say goodbye to your old life and hello to a new one. You know that."

"I do. But sometimes, like tonight, when I have too much time on my hands, I start feeling a little guilty. It's just so hard. If I move forward, I'm confirming the past is behind me. And I don't know how I can do that." She stopped, not daring to say another word for fear of letting a sob loose.

He knew. So he chose to move the conversation into a different direction. "You have to move forward when you have the chance. This happened because you're ready. I know you may have doubts. I'm sure he does, too. But the fact you two have come so far says a lot. It says you're ready. You're ready to move on, to move forward. And if that means together, if it works for the both of you, all the better."

"I feel it when we're together. But being alone like this, it scares me back into second guessing myself. I feel like a yo-yo."

"Two steps forward, one step back. You may have tough times along this road. But honestly, I think it's got to be easier being with Aiden. He's been there too. You know what you've both been through. You get that part of each other." Chris knew he didn't understand completely. But he could imagine.

"You're right. Of course, you're right. And I do know. It's like I just need you to tell me. To be that little voice that tells me it's all okay. I don't know why I need that, but I do. Thanks for being that voice."

"Anytime."

Kelly thought back to her week with Aiden. So many good times. So many memories. She'd been replaying them over and over in her mind. This thing between them was far from being over. She knew it had only begun. *If she could just talk to him ...*

Chris broke into her thoughts.

"So, let's make a list. That's what you want to do, isn't it?"

Oh, he knew her so well.

"First, make your plans for after he returns. Email him again. Say you're sorry if you feel the need. Agree to meet and talk. Does he know you'll be in San Diego?"

She sighed. "Nope. I think I spoke of it a couple of times, but I never got into the details."

"So get into the details. Make a plan. Get things out in the open. At least you'll know where you stand."

"Done. I'll start writing as soon as we hang up."

"Second, move forward. You've got a few weeks, right? So use them. Pack up boxes. Clean up your rooms. Paint if you have to. Do what feels right, okay?"

"Already in action. I made a list of things I want to accomplish on the plane. I bought more boxes today when I was out running errands."

Chris laughed. "Now why doesn't that surprise me?"

Kelly snickered. "Hey. I had to go out anyway. Might as well do two things at once." She could see her brother shaking his head.

Chris shook the humor from his voice, grew serious and continued, "Third and most importantly, don't do anything you're not ready for. Trust yourself, okay? It's worked so far. You're doing good." He took a deep breath. "I'm proud of you. I love you, you know that, right?"

"Yep. Me, too."

Kelly closed her eyes, breathed deep. Slowly, she felt the past push down inside her and the present come back. The feeling she had this past week when she'd been with Aiden.

And as if he could sense the change, Chris broke into her thoughts once again.

"So this is serious."

"Yeah, I think it is. But we've only been together under the very best circumstances. Meeting each other for a vacation isn't real life. We need to be together. We need to live together. Have life's ups and downs together, you know? We need to see each other in daily routines, spend time with our families and friends. That's what's next. That's what we need to see if all of this will work."

"I really need to meet him."

She laughed. "Chris, I love you. Thanks for being my big brother."

"Any time, baby. Now can I get back to sleep? Can we talk when normal people are up?"

"Goodnight."

Chapter Fifty-Five

From: Kelly
Subject: I miss you already
To: Aiden

I've written this email several dozen times. I finish, read it, hit delete. Over and over again.

I've poured out my heart and soul. Delete.

I've tried to explain. Delete.

I've told you my feelings. Delete.

I've tried to justify. Delete.

I've told stories. Delete.

LORI OSTERBERG

I've babbled on and on. Delete.

And finally, I realized I don't need to go on and on.

The two nights here in Portland brought me back to life. Your emails ignited my soul. Our week together in Vietnam taught me all I needed to know.

I want you in my life. I want to learn more.

I may not have been ready to tell you what you needed to hear. This is my path, and I need to do it in my own way. It doesn't mean I don't feel the same way. It simply means I'm not ready to say it in the way you did.

I need closure before I can open a new door. I need to put some things behind me before I move on.

I'd like to talk about us.

I'm keynoting at the Romance Writers Association in San Diego the last three days of September. I know you're back a few days before. Can we meet the first of October and work things out?

Kelly

Chapter Fifty-Six

From: Aiden
Subject: I miss you more
To: Kelly

From the time I booked the trip to Vietnam, I'd thought about the day we'd have to say goodbye. I'd wondered what would happen in our ten days together. Who we'd become. What we'd want for our futures. And how difficult it would be to leave if we found out we had something special.

Goodbye killed me.

Partially because I was kicking myself, trying to come up with the right words. In the best of times, I'm not great at communicating. And knowing I wouldn't see you again for weeks, it simply took everything I had not to grab you and run.

You're right. We need closure to our old lives before we move forward. We each need to do that on our own.

Yes, I'll be back permanently on the twentieth of September. Yes, I want to see you in October. Yes, I want to see who we are together.

Until then, I'm giving us both the space we need for all of this.

Just know you'll never be out of my thoughts.

Because I love you.

Aiden

Chapter Fifty-Seven

Kelly dug in and worked.

Chance Encounters almost composed itself. She'd felt it when she wrote *Finding Love Again* after Tom had died. She felt it equally with *Chance Encounters*. In less than two weeks, she went from mapping it out to writing a seventy thousand word novel.

Her editor loved the story and made very few changes. Her publicist continued booking a tightly woven book tour across the United States for the late fall. Her designer moved quickly to get the book designed, formatted, and ready for release in the online world.

A few days before her flight to San Diego, she released it to rave reviews.

"Another best seller from the expert at midlife romance."
"Best. Book. Ever."

"I laughed. I cried. I cheered. I gifted copies for my closest friends so that we could talk about Jennifer and Dane's love affair."

"Where can I find my own Dane Masters?"

While writing consumed her business hours, Kelly found herself equally as enthusiastic about her personal life.

She packed up all of Tom's things. She kept a few things she'd cherish forever, let her daughter choose what meant most to her. Then together they'd boxed up the rest and given it away. Difficult didn't describe the emotion that flowed through her as she said goodbye once more.

But in some ways, it had been easier than she'd feared.

Perhaps it was because she had motivation for her future. She had someone there, on the other side, doing the exact same things.

They hadn't emailed. They hadn't spoken. Somehow she knew he was there. That he was processing and doing the right things he needed to do to move forward.

She'd sent only one additional email; a copy of *Chance Encounters*. He inspired it. The characters were driven by their time together. She wanted him to read it.

Fully packed and ready to go, she made her way to the airport.

Portland's airport was easy to maneuver. Kelly wove through the security line, stopped and picked up a coffee before making her way to the gate.

"Hey, you." Beth snagged her arm around Kelly's waist and brought her in for a hug. She pulled her to the corner where she had staked out a spot near the window.

THE WRITER

Kelly looked at the papers and equipment Beth had spread out all over. "Looks like you've moved in," she said with a raise of an eyebrow.

Beth shrugged, "I've been here an hour already. Todd dropped me off early so he could get back for a meeting."

"We could have taken Uber together."

Beth shook her head. "No. Todd and I did lunch first. I won't see him for a week."

Kelly nodded. She remembered what that was like, trying to fit in time for each other not because you had to, but because you wanted to.

"So are you ready?"

"Of course. I could keynote in my sleep. And Q&As are always easy. There're a couple of new writers I'm interested in meeting too. And eMotions Book Marketing is there. They do that large book fair in Florida in the spring; I'd love to get in on that," she trailed off as she saw Beth's head shaking back and forth.

"That's not what I meant, and you know it." Beth tipped her head, waiting for a response.

Kelly fell back into her chair, contemplating her next words.

Of course, she'd thought about it a lot. She'd imagined every scenario possible.

Her and Aiden talking. Her and Aiden fighting. Her and Aiden moving forward. Her and Aiden saying goodbye.

One way or another, she was going to be okay. She'd made peace with her past. Was ready for the future. Life was good. And she was ready to move on.

Possibly with Aiden.

But before she met with him, she had to get through the convention.

She looked Beth in the eye. "I love him. I haven't said it to him. But I know it. You know it. He knows it too if he'd think about it. But that doesn't change the fact that I need my space. I needed to do this on my time. I still do. And how that works out for the two of us, together, now that he's home, we'll just have to see."

Kelly got lost in feeling him beside her, close, the way they were inside the airport in Vietnam that first morning. She could feel him even though he wasn't beside her. She moved her hands over her arms.

Beth moved in and hugged her once again. "You don't have to say another word. I get it all. It'll work out. It will."

They sat and talked about everything and nothing. They made their way onto the plane, settled in for a two-hour flight.

Kelly popped in her earbuds and selected the playlist she'd created for the book. Then, she dug in answering emails and creating posts for social sites.

And she planned.

With the conference over on Wednesday, she'd tacked on a few extra days to the end, planning on staying through the weekend. He goal was to connect with Aiden and see if he'd meet her just to talk.

She replayed her intentions over and over, trying to think of every outcome. Would he be willing to talk? Would they move forward? Or would they say goodbye forever?

There were some things she just couldn't think about. That was one of them.

Releasing Tom from her heart had almost killed her. A part of him would always be there. But he wasn't with her anymore to bring her the daily interaction she craved.

She wanted conversation. She wanted the day to day rituals that came from truly being with one another. She wanted someone by her side. Not necessarily living with her day to day. But someone she cared about, thought about. Loved.

She thought about Aiden in the restaurant, the walk back to her home, his first kiss. He had her mesmerized. Then his emails. His wit, his charm, his honesty. She knew she'd never had learned that much about him face to face. The way he wrote said a lot more than the words he used when they were together. Being together had sealed the deal.

She thought she loved him then. She didn't tell him. But she knew it in her heart.

When he said it, she knew she felt it too. But she wanted to be free from the past before she gave that kind of commitment to anyone. And frankly, the marriage thing scared her. Still did. Would she ever get to that point again? She didn't know. But she did know one thing. Whatever had started between them wasn't over in her mind.

She knew it now. She knew she wanted more. She wanted him. Because she loved him. But would it be too late?

He'd said he was ready to move forward. He didn't need time to think. Yet he'd had a lot of it these past few weeks.

Was he ready to give them a try? Or was he ready to move on?

She went through the motions of giving her keynote, signing books, posing with fans for pictures. She smiled and took it all in graciously. These were her fans, and she appreciated them more than anything. They'd been there with her through the thick of it all. She owed them a lot.

But somewhere in the back of her mind was the thought of her new life.

What did the future hold?

Would it include Aiden? Would it include San Diego?

She loved talking with her fans. Especially with her new release still so fresh in everyone's minds.

The countdown had begun.

Three more days. Two more nights. One day until she would call him and see where they stood.

She woke early and got ready for her last day of the convention.

She loved the final few hours. There was something emotional about it, where friends came together for the last time before making their way back home. In just a few short years, she'd made a lot of friends in the writing industry. Leaving always took a lot of time.

And this year, with all of her successes behind her, she'd been scheduled for the last presentation. A group Q&A session with two other successful writers.

She made her way to the front of the room. They were briefed on the format, fitted with microphones, and led to the stage where they were introduced to a loud round of applause.

In some ways, she liked Q&A sessions the best. She'd get honest with her fans. She could reveal little details about her life, the way she wrote, what motivated her, what gave her inspiration. She loved the questions her fans asked. And here with two other women, she'd learn a thing or two about their writing processes as well.

She listened as the moderator read the bios, talked about their books, introduced them to the crowd.

And it began.

"Who's your favorite character?"
"What does a writing day look like for you?"
"How long does it take you to write a book?"

THE WRITER

"What's your favorite book?"
"What advice would you give a brand new writer?"

The moderator dug in and distributed a few questions to each author.

They spoke. They shared. They laughed.

Kelly listened to each fan carefully and answered as thoroughly as she could. She knew a lot of them were attempting to find their own fame in the writing world. She wanted to give them an honest look at what a writer's life was like.

The moderator went back and forth through the audience, attempting to get to everyone that had a question. He moved fast. And they'd all agreed to answer as quickly as possible to get as much information out.

Kelly saw the hand pop up. She saw the moderator make his way over to her. She smiled.

Beth.

"I loved *Finding Love Again*. That one spoke to me. And while I adored all of your books, *Finding Love Again* seems different. Where did you find your inspiration for it?" She looked at her expectantly as she stood behind the microphone, with just a hint of mischief in her eyes.

I can play this game. Kelly knew Beth was up to something, so she answered honestly. "Almost four years ago, my husband Tom and I embarked on a new journey. We uprooted our lives, sold off our family home, and moved from San Francisco to Portland to try something new. Two years in, Tom was killed in a car accident." Kelly paused. She heard the hush rumble across the audience. It always did. She took a breath, gathered her emotions. It was getting easier, but it was always there.

She looked back out, made eye contact with Beth. "I lost my world when that happened. Tom and I had a midlife love affair going on. We fell in love all over again as we faced our empty nest, just the two of us. We had so many plans, so many dreams." She breathed deep. "And in an instant, it was over."

"I died that day." She said it quietly, but the room was equally as quiet, taking in her words. She took it up a notch, her voice stronger than it'd been a long while.

"But I'm a glass-half-full kind of gal. I've always been the one who screams 'live life to the fullest.' So about three months after it happened, I woke up with a story in my head. I got up and started writing. And in less than three weeks, *Finding Love Again* was finished. To say it was a labor of love would be an understatement. But the story came so naturally to me. The words flowed. I couldn't stop typing. I worked eighteen-hour days. It flowed. I edited it a couple of times myself. And by the time I got it to my editor's, she barely needed to change a thing.

"*Finding Love Again* was my therapy. It brought me back to life. It allowed me to clear old wounds, say what I needed to say. I released it, and it swept like wildfire. It's been on a variety of bestseller lists; the reviews are out of this world." Kelly paused one more time. She knew her fellow writers well. She scanned across the audience, meeting many sets of eyes that were peering out at her, watching, listening.

"As writers, it's often hard to distinguish between fiction and reality. Sure, we make up the stories. But it's all built around who we are, what experiences we've had, how we've faced our own lives. We all know that every one of our characters has a little piece of who we are inside. Or maybe who we want to be. It's fun to live our fantasies out in our books, isn't it, ladies?" She waited for the chuckle to fill the room.

"And for me, this book in some way helped me say I was alive, no matter what my life circumstances had been. It was okay for me to go on. I would be fine. It allowed me to take the next step in my life, and it made all the difference. It's led to a few more great books. It's led me to great friendships. And a chance at building a new life again."

The applause went on and on. Kelly saw more than one woman dabbing at their eyes.

But in her heart, she was fine. She'd learned she was ready to put it in the past. She'd learned she'd be okay. More than okay. She was ready to love again.

And as she saw the moderator motioning for quiet and the audience returning to their seats, she saw Beth grab the microphone one more time.

Beth wasn't done. She took to the microphone once again.

"So *Finding Love Again* was your therapy. Does your new book *Chance Encounters* have personal meaning as well?"

Kelly shook her head at her friend.

"Beth, Beth, Beth." Kelly chuckled as she pointed back towards where Beth was standing. "Everyone, this is my dear friend Beth Watson, a fellow romance writer. I wouldn't have survived the loss of my husband without this woman. And now she's setting me up because she knows the ending of the story." She turned her head and roamed across the audience. "Want to hear?"

Of course, everyone in the audience shouted YES. Those who followed her regularly on her blog or Facebook had already read parts of the story. She knew there were an equal number of women in the audience who were meeting her for the first time.

And so she'd tell it. Again. That was a part of this story. That's how she marketed it. And it was working well so far.

"*Chance Encounters* looks at how a split decision can change the course of your life forever. By doing one thing, changing your mind about one thing, how it can cause a ripple effect that will impact all of your relationships for the rest of your life. And yes, it holds a very personal meaning for me." Her eyes found Beth, and they shared a smile.

"Four months ago, Beth made it her mission to have me start living again. And on one particular night, she dragged me out of my home and to a restaurant to enjoy a beautiful night in Portland, right during the middle of the Rose Festival. Fleet Week coincides with the Rose Festival, bringing several ships into port and releasing hundreds of gorgeous Naval men and women into the streets of Portland." She stopped for effect. "Yeah, it's a good week."

The crowd erupted in laughter.

"After an hour wait, my friend noticed two gentlemen, two captains, giving their names to the host, facing their own hour wait. And she made a split decision that changed my life forever. One of the captains was also widowed, having lost his wife to cancer just a few days after my husband's death. The connection was instant. The attraction was ..." She let her eyes scan the crowd. "Sizzling."

Kelly let the audience quiet down.

"After two days, he set sail. And our romance blossomed through email. We've met in Vietnam for ten days. And the captain returned here to San Diego a week ago."

And that's where the story ended ... for the moment. But she kept the story alive. After all, this was a romance convention.

Quietly, she continued, "Sometimes life is best lived by taking full advantage of chance encounters. I've learned that life is way too short. And if we don't watch for the little opportunities that are everywhere, we're likely to miss out on some of the greatest moments of life. Life is meant to enjoy. It's meant to live with zeal. It's meant to be filled with passion. And yes, to

THE WRITER

be filled with romance. I plan on living my life to the fullest, and I wish the same for every one of you. Thanks, everybody."

Kelly waved out to her audience. This was what she loved most about what she did. She loved telling stories, this process of bringing hope to others, sharing courage to others that were facing their own challenging situations. This is what she truly loved to do.

The session came to an end. She followed the moderator to a table in the back already filled with her books. The line wrapped back towards the stage with fans wanting books signed. And she settled in for a couple of hours of signing books, posing for photos, and chatting with women that all had a story to tell.

You get me.
You helped me recover.
You helped me when I was down.
You made me look at love differently.
You gave me hope.
You're my inspiration.

Those words kept her going. They kept her writing. And they would for a very long time.

Chapter Fifty-Eight

Deciding patience was not at the top of his priority list, Aiden chose to run up the stairs rather than standing behind dozens of women on the escalator.

He'd never felt more out of place as he made his way through a sea of women laughing and talking about everything romance. Clearly, he hadn't thought this all the way through when he'd decided to come straight from work. His dress whites did little to help him blend in. In fact, they caused quite a stir.

He'd never been to a book convention. And he was quickly coming to the conclusion that a romance book convention had a little too much estrogen for comfort. He was wishing he was any other place as he climbed the stairs and felt dozens of pairs of eyes on him. The whispering was all around him.

But he couldn't wait any longer. She was here, and he was going to see her. Today.

He waited patiently in line at the help desk.

He knew she spoke today. Still, the website hadn't revealed the details he truly needed to know. The when and where that would lead him to her.

So he waited, minute after minute, as the line slowly moved towards the window.

"May I help you?"

Aiden walked up to the counter. "Hi, I'm trying to find what room Kelly Sorenson is speaking in."

"Do you have admission?" She eyed him warily.

"No." He hadn't thought of that. "She's my girlfriend." As if that said it all. They still had to work out all of the details. He hoped she'd back him up and support the statement if she were asked.

The woman behind the counter continued to look skeptical. "I'm sorry. We can't let you in on the show floor without admission. And you won't have access to where Ms. Sorenson is speaking without getting onto the show floor."

"Can I purchase a ticket? Is there a way? I know this is the last day. I'm supposed to meet her here."

Sure, he was stretching the truth. But he was desperate to see her.

"Hold on a minute." The woman moved out of sight, presumably to check with a supervisor.

He tapped his finger and looked around, trying to wait patiently.

"Aiden?"

He glanced to the side. "Beth? Hi."

Beth moved to the front of the line and drew him into a quick hug. "What are you doing here?"

"I have to see her. I'm just trying to get them to let me in."

Beth could see the desperation in his eyes. She glanced at her watch.

THE WRITER

"She just finished her last session. She's signing books now."

"Yeah. I knew she spoke today. I figured I'd find her and see her when I could. But they won't let me in."

"Aiden, you're sure about this?" Beth narrowed her eyes, taking him in. "You want to take this step? Because I will do anything to keep Kelly safe. You know that, right?"

Aiden didn't want to talk about all of this with Beth. But he understood her concerns.

"I wouldn't be here if I wasn't sure." He met her eyes and held steady.

She nodded, satisfied with his response.

Beth felt her matchmaking skills come to life once again. She'd done it once before for the two of them. She'd do it again, today. And after the questions she'd just asked her best friend in her presentation, she knew this would be icing on the cake. This was a romance expo after all.

So she asked him, "Who were you talking to?"

Aiden pointed to the woman down at the end, talking with another woman.

Beth made her way down to the farthest window where she could speak to the women in charge.

"Excuse me; you were helping the gentleman down on the end?"

One nodded.

"I know him. He is with Kelly Sorenson. He's just back in town and didn't plan on being here. But he wanted to surprise her here today. Is there any way you can let him in? You can take down my name if you need to." Beth looked expectantly at them, hoping to convince them. "It's the last day. He wanted to be here to help her pack up her booth."

That did it. They went into motion, grabbed him a badge and took down his information.

A few moments later, Beth ushered him down towards the presentation hall.

With a crowded line wrapped around the book signing tables, Beth found a group of women and tucked Aiden behind them. Kelly would have several more fans to talk with before coming face to face with Aiden. A brief explanation had the women more than willing to participate and hide him until the right moment.

He moved forward, inching along. He loved watching her work. Listening to stories. Signing a book. Posing for a picture. Giving a warm hug. She was in her element. It was clear to him that she loved what she did.

And she was good at it. He'd never been to a book signing and had nothing to judge it against. But he could tell she enjoyed it just by watching her. She connected with every single person that stepped up to her table. She didn't rush them. She listened and watched. She smiled. She gave her all.

And that, that was what he decided he loved the most.

Without realizing it until now, it was that fact that had completely done him in. She gave everything. No questions. No expectations. She gave.

When she listened to him, she was fully present.

When she spoke with him, there was no one else in the room.

When she laughed with him, she was genuine.

When she loved him, she gave her all.

And that was what she had said when they left Vietnam together.

He'd heard, but he hadn't understood until this very moment. She had to give her all. She had to be one hundred per-

THE WRITER

cent in. And with so many loose ends back home, she couldn't do that. So she wouldn't.

When she committed, she'd give her all. Or nothing.

And with her Tom's life still entwined with her own, she didn't have one hundred percent to give. She'd wanted to clean things up. She'd wanted to say goodbye. Goodbye to the past. Hello to the future. That was all.

And he'd been dumb enough to think that she wanted to look for something more. He was grateful he'd finally woken up. It now made perfect sense. He was also grateful her words had helped him make changes of his own, like cleaning out his wife's belongings, getting a decorator to redo his bedroom. He'd had the opportunity to tell Michelle how much he'd loved her, but it was finally time to leave her in the past. How grateful he was for her in his life, for making him who he was right now. For giving him permission to move on.

He was ready.

For her. For Kelly.

And he'd wait for this woman in front of him, no matter how long it took.

The line moved. Slowly the women got what they came for and moved on.

She looked tired, yet energized. He knew how much she'd given, imagined how tiring it must be.

She didn't see what was around her, instead focused solely on each person as they stepped up to the table.

So he stood in line and waited his turn.

Kelly took a sip of water from her water bottle and moved it back off to the side. She traded out a few pens, moved a few more books closer to her.

She was dying for a chance to stand up and walk for a minute. She was dying for a meal.

Hell, she was dying for a bathroom break.

She wiggled a little, adjusting her body so she could talk with more women.

"Hi, Kelly, I'm Sara. Your books have been a lifeline for me." And off she went again, spending a few minutes connecting with another fan.

She signed. She chatted. She shared. She did what she did best.

The hall was getting louder, filled with laughter and loud voices. And while she enjoyed the interactions, she was more than ready to move on. She had one thought on her mind: Aiden. She wanted more than ever to talk with him once again. She tried to stay focused. She tried her best to give each person the attention she deserved.

"Hi, Kelly, I'm Nancy ..."

"I'm Grace ..."

"I'm Barb ..."

The smile. The story. The little hug that said thank you. The pose for a photo.

She returned to her seat, grabbed a pen and looked at the next person in line.

And caught her breath when she saw who it was. Their eyes held for a moment.

Did the hall just get quieter, or is that me?

He looked even more fantastic than she'd remembered. His eyes. His smile. His ... everything. Kelly didn't think anything could look better than a man dressed in white. Especially when that man was one named Captain Aiden Maddock.

He was here. He was standing in front of her.

THE WRITER

While every part of her wanted to jump up from her chair and climb him like a tree, attach her lips to his for a very long time, a small little piece told her to wait. Take your time. Find out why he's here.

She glanced at the line behind her, suddenly quiet and watching expectantly.

She looked back to the next person in line. Aiden.

She held out her hand. "Where's your book?"

He raised his eyebrows. "Book?"

"Yes, you're in the book signing line. I'll sign your book." Her eyes danced as she watched him.

"Um ..." He'd been rehearsing all kinds of ways to start the conversation. *Where's your book* had never factored into his thoughts.

"What? No book? What am I going to sign?" She bit her lip to keep from smiling at his puzzled look.

"I don't know. I hadn't thought that far."

"You can buy one. I have one right here." She reached into a pile and brought out a copy of her latest release.

"Perfect. I'll take it," he said smiling, clearly ready to play.

"And who do I make it out to?" She looked at him expectantly. Stared into his eyes, not sure if she'd ever be able to look away again.

Aiden put his hands down on the table, leaned in so he was inches from her face.

"You choose. Say what you have to say."

Her eyes watched his as the fire began to burn. She moved down, watching his lips as she began to quiver.

Composure. Just give me a little self-control, please.

She knew if she touched him, she'd lose it completely. And with a long line left behind him, that simply wasn't an option.

She leaned over the book scribbled furiously for a few seconds. Closed it. Put the pen down. Picked the book up off the table and held it out to him.

A clever smirk spread across his face.

"I want a photo too."

Shit.

He turned to the group behind him, swiped at his phone and asked if they'd take the picture.

He moved to the side, waiting for her to stand up. And as she did, he snaked an arm around her waist, pulled her into him and held her close. He breathed her in. And almost to himself, "I missed you. I miss us."

Fuck composure.

She grabbed his face between her palms and pulled him in. She tasted. They touched. She couldn't get enough. She felt herself shoot out into orbit.

The whooping and hollering of the nearby crowd brought her back down to earth.

"Um ..." Clearly breathless, clearly embarrassed, she looked out at the women remaining in the line.

She pulled herself together, looked at the man beside her, and stated to her crowd, "He does that to me every time. I mean, look at him!" She swatted at him affectionately.

The crowd ate it up.

If anything, her line got longer after the little show they'd put on. The ruckus pulled people in from the passing hallway. She sold out of books in just a few minutes.

She continued to sign while Aiden hovered by her side. Watched her. Supported her. Waited.

When the last fan left the floor, she stood and turned to him.

She studied him. "Why are you here? Why did you come today?"

THE WRITER

"I'm sorry. I'm sorry for pushing so hard that last morning. I'm sorry for giving you little option. I should have handled that better, and I just wanted to tell you that in person."

She shook her head as he talked. "You don't have to be sorry for the way you feel. But at the same time, understand that I needed time. I still do."

He nodded and grabbed her hands. "I get that. I understand. I think I was just so overwhelmed at everything, and the thought of not seeing you made me a little crazy. I saw so much happening in my future, and you were in it. I just didn't want to let go."

She thought about that for a moment. "Okay. I am enjoying whatever this is growing between us. But you have to realize that my timeline may be different than yours. I'm not going to change that for you or anybody. I like my life in many ways, and I don't want to make significant changes that I might regret later. Slow still works for me. I need slow to see how this all falls into place."

He smiled as he pulled her closer. "I want you. I need you. I love you. I just want more. Whatever that means. We can go slow. We can go fast. I'm happy either way."

His eyes watched her expectantly. And everything she'd been thinking seemed to fall to the side. He did that to her. He drove her wild. He made her feel whole again.

She wanted him. Whether that meant now, for a while, or for the rest of their lives, she no longer cared.

One day at a time.

It worked. She wanted it. She'd take it and live it for all it was worth.

She wanted him.

He moved his hands up by the side of her face. Tucked a stand of hair behind her ear. Moved in closer and said it again.

"I love you, Kelly. Nothing's going to change that." He kissed her gently. "I know you feel it too."

He held the book up. Opened it to the first page where she had signed her name a short while before.

To the man that took my breath away from the moment I saw him.

I love you.

Kelly

She did. She loved him. What else was there?

Just three little words conveyed all she felt. With three little words, she could give him what he needed to know.

"I love you." She smiled.

She watched as a world of emotion passed through him.

They could figure the rest out as they moved forward. They could take it one day at a time.

But for now, he was hers. Aiden and Kelly.

They had just become us. They were together. And she planned on enjoying every moment of it.

ABOUT THE AUTHOR

After running several successful businesses, Lori Osterberg decided it was time to reinvent herself once again. Facing an empty nest and too much normal suburbia lifestyle in front of her, she talked her husband into selling off their 3300 square foot home, sell two-thirds of their stuff, all for the chance to slow travel the world. When not traveling, she finds a friend or two to share a good bottle of wine, visits tea factories, dances the night away at outdoor concerts, eats her way through farmers markets, and daydreams about the next set of characters she lives vicariously through. She's currently writing books and living the dream in the Pacific Northwest.

You can learn more at:
http://LoriOsterberg.com
Lori on Twitter: @LoriOsterberg
Lori on Facebook: facebook.com/TheChoiceBooks

Made in the USA
Monee, IL
17 October 2020